SORROWS' EDGE

"G R R R R R"

Ryan L Robinson

Word Art Publishing
9350 Wilshire Blvd
Suite 203, Beverly Hills, CA 90212
www.wordartpublishing.com
Phone: 1 (888) 614 - 1370

Published by Word Art Publishing

ISBN: Paperback   978-1-955070-27-0
       Hardback   978-1-955070-28-7
       Ebook   978-1-955070-29-4

This book is dedicated to:

My Family for putting up with my nonsense.

Kay, JoAnn, Eleanor, and Penny.

The ones who have fallen; Bob, Vivian, Jan and Hal.

Special thanks to Vivian Prince for her artwork on the Lizards.

To Tree, for making it much better.

FORWARD

Humanity has been, as we say, "on top of the food chain," for a long time. We didn't have many big bad predators to fight or compete with. So, we fought ourselves instead. And put each other in boxes, categories, lists, stigmas, and cages. How stupid we have been.

Someday we may not be the bad-est beasts on the block. We may have to learn lessons we are not prepared for. But we will learn them, one way or another. The caveat is, can we survive the future lessons of life? Can we be strong or compassionate or understanding when we need to be? Will we have the wit to escape or even deal with our dilemmas? As the old song goes, "teach your children well." Our future survival may depend on it.

The story you're about to read, is of course, totally fiction. I wrote it to explore some of these ideas and have fun. I hope you have fun and maybe, take some time to think.

CHAPTER 1

"Namaste."

The soft greeting brought the consciousness of morning to Jerry. He slowly awakened to what he heard. Something struck him as different. In the dim light of the room smiling green eyes studied him through strands of reddish-brown hair. He wasn't alone. This neither surprised nor shocked him. He liked it.

From beneath a sea of white silky sheets a slender hand emerged and swept away soft curls to reveal a face that he could only imagine belonged to an angel. She slid next to him. To his delight, neither one had anything on.

"Hi, who are you?" he asked.

"I'm Angelica-So," she replied.

"Have we met before?" He asked with a grin.

Her fist jabbed into his ribs. She laughed at his groan. "We were married yesterday."

"Yes, as a matter of fact, I do remember something about a ceremony." Shifting his weight, he slipped his forearm beneath her head and smooth hair. Looking down at her he couldn't envisage a more perfect place to be.

"And don't you forget it," she added.

He couldn't believe how beautiful this creature looked and how wonderful he felt. No, he would never forget. Their lips gently met as they melted together.

*   *   *

Thomas McCormick couldn't have felt better. In the last two years things had really come together and his political ambitions were realized. The party was more of a quiet celebration with his friends and the people who had helped him the most in his election. They were enjoying themselves. The space in his apartment wasn't small by local standards but crowded with happy humans.

It was not just his victory, but theirs as well. They had collectively and peaceably elected him as their Representative. A person to stand for the planet at the Union. Nearly half the human race, scattered across the lower Arm, had access to representation and they were included.

His wife, Elizabeth-Charm, played the perfect hostess. He watched her gracefully move around the room and mingle with their guests. This made him aware of how fortunate a man could be. He realized that over the last few weeks she had worked harder than anyone on his campaign. Maybe more than him. Perhaps he should send her off to Ichorous to represent the people, and he could stay home to relax. Truly, they both were Representatives of Mitzul. He vowed to take the time to do something to express his appreciation for her sacrifice over the past few months. No, it wouldn't have happened without her, and he hadn't appreciated her enough.

As if this hadn't been abundant good fortune, their son had left for his advanced learning a few days ago. Good things were happening everywhere.

"Thomas," came a voice from behind, "we moved a lot of rock to make this happen."

"I'm sorry, Armondo. I'm still trying to figure out what happened," he said to his old friend. "We were born in a cold cave. And now look at us."

"Nothing hard to understand," said Armondo. "Our fathers came here when this was nothing more than a half a shaft of worthless ore. Along with a bunch of other crazy people, we turned Mitzul into an almost decent world to live in."

"You make it sound so easy and matter of fact."

"We're mining a dozen different ores. We have good profitability and standard of living. Just look at our homes. There is nothing 'new-colony' about anything here. And, think of it, in a couple a hundred years or so, the terra forming on the surface will make the atmosphere almost breathable. To top it all off, we have a newly elected

Representative to the Union." Armondo smiled and put his hand on his friends' shoulder.

"You ticked those off like you were the politician," Thomas smiled. "Don't get me wrong. I do understand. We should never take this for granted. We've worked twice as hard to get half as much as any other species. It makes everything that much sweeter."

"Are you boring our guest again, dear?" Charm smiled, as she stepped up and slipped her arm around his waist.

"Just practicing making boring speeches for when we get to Ichorous," he replied.

"I'm so looking forward to that," Charm said.

"What, me making boring speeches?"

"No. We haven't been off the planet together for so long. And to be on Ichorous again will be wonderful. Just think we can walk outside without an environmental suit. Look up at the stars peeking through the clouds and breath natural air." Charm spoke mostly to Armondo. Thomas had heard this many times before and this was her opportunity to bend Armondos' ear on the subject.

Thomas wanted to share all these marvelous sights with Charm. There were too few places where humans could leave the cave and feel the natural elements on their face.

"You two are going to love it. But tell me, have you heard from that beautiful sister of yours?" Armondo asked.

"Yes, we have. Angelica-So is getting married. In fact, she might be by now."

"You're kidding. She actually fell for that gravel pusher she found in a hole on . . . what was the name of that rock?"

"Bohica." Elizabeth-Charm snapped with a look of distaste. "You're just jealous because you and Angelica didn't hit it off as you hoped."

"That could be."

"Don't let him fool you," Thomas broke in. "I told him all about that before. And I think he doesn't care because he's seeing someone."

"Really? You must tell us all about her."

"I swear, there's no one. Thomas is now fooling you."

The entrance door signaled.

"Another guest." Thomas said.

"Maybe it's the Governor." Charm squeezed his arm with excitement.

Thomas excused himself with a big smile on his face. Rumors had circulated that he might show up. Even though the Governor of Mitzul had supported another candidate for the position, it would be politically advantageous to show a united front.

Opening the door startled Thomas. He staggered backwards. Standing before him was a large, ash grey, soft skin and tailless lizard. Although it could stand upright under human high ceilings, it had to stoop to get its head through the doorway. The reason for the awkwardness was six sharp horns coming from the side of its head, turning at right angles and sticking straight up. It only wore a translator on its hip.

The room became quiet, and all attention turned to this foreboding form as its flashing red eyes fixed on its host.

*   *   *

Jerry woke again in the dim room, this time to a com signal beeping. He got up and made his way to the desk across the small cluttered room. The cramped quarters were typical in the new mining colony. Humans arrived only eight months ago and immediately began to tunnel into the barren lifeless planet of Bohica. Still undressed, he keyed the small device for voice only.

"Jerry, is that you? This is Hank at the Administration Center."

"Go away."

"Sorry, but the CA wants everyone in a meeting in ten minutes."

"Can't it wait? You know I'm on my honeymoon."

"We need you here."

"Hell, you do. I've earned this time off. Get someone else, Hank."

"Afraid not. You're it. We have four ships converging on Bohica each from a different direction. They are big and have a threatening posture. Decidedly unfriendly. I'll bet you anything they're Fire Lizards."

"Come on, they're not going to try anything. We have a treaty to mine this worthless rock. We've seen them buzzing around before. They want to make sure we know that they are the boss in this part of the universe. When they get tired, they'll go home. Posturing is very important to them. Besides, it doesn't sound like the kind of tactics they'd use for a hostile move."

"Please, Jerry. Everything is going crazy. You may be right, but work has stopped. Some people want to evacuate. There's even a small riot at the arms locker. You've got to get up here Jerry, everyone trusts you. Help us control the situation."

Jerry took a moment to rub his eyes. "I'll be there."

He turned around and saw Angelica sitting up in bed. She heard, but would she understand if he left? He didn't want to leave her, not ever.

*　　*　　*

The Tri-Bah Group Master stood in an empty room on his flagship, the *Inner Stone*. A gentle hum, ship noise, kept the room from silence. He looked out the window at one of his other ships. The Cluster Class war ship could be seen in its entirety with the dark expanse salted with stars, all frozen in a surreal image. He loved these moments of serenity.

There were no decisions to make or orders to give. And yet everyone in his command continued to do their jobs in a seamless activity. He didn't have to tell the mechanic to fix the machine or the cook to prepare a meal. Others took care of that. He enjoyed his position, the responsibility and the power that came with it. That continued to be the meaning of his life.

When he began training, many years ago, he learned that the more chaos you create the more order you need. So, he relished the balance in these quiet times in between the hectic moments of the universe.

He ran the two opposable thumbs of his right paw under his chin and considered the events that brought him here. The consequences of what he did today weigh on his mind. There were too many unknowns for his comfort. As the executor of policy for his race, duty could be difficult. Not that he felt threatened or obligated to any other species within any sector around him.

Other races called them Fire Lizards. He mused at the name. They really didn't breathe fire that was just a myth told to frighten ignorant creatures. The name came from their coloration. Their thin muscular legs and lower torso were a deep rich brown. At mid-chest their body turned reddish, then into a pure red, and blending into orange and shades of yellows at the shoulders. From the neck up, they were bright yellow. Except, of course for the three distinctive black spots on their forehead. They were a living caricature of a burning stick.

A formation of three small Pebble Fighters gently moved between the two ships. The Group Master knew they had returned from patrol. Allowing himself pride at these quiet moments always lifted his spirits. There were many other fleets belonging to the Tri-Bah but there was no finer group for him to command. They were the dominant force to be dealt with in this part of the galactic arm.

Another had entered the room. It smelled different. A species of lizards with dark marbled green skin, a large jaw with small sharp teeth and yellow eyes came to destroy his serenity. It looked smug in its black tunic with gold trim.

"All has gone well, Admiral," it said.

"So, I have heard."

"I watched it happen. The timing was all within nominal. The geometry could not have been better. The data we received has been exceptional. It turned out to be quite a spectacle."

"A very expensive one." The Group Master's mood turned dark. "I'm still not convinced that this demonstration is worth the cost. More conventional methods would have worked well. It might have taken longer, but I'm not aware of any timetable. Also, the impact would have been lessened, making the follow-up negotiations easier."

The tall Green lizard crossed his arms, curving long slender claws over his shoulders. The Group Master recognized this defensive stance.

"Your superiors made that decision and took that responsibility. You were instructed to carry out their directives. And now we can move forward."

"Can we?" Group Master felt a little manipulated.

"You have some doubt?"

"Yes. There will be much activity by them to understand the significance of this event."

"We are expecting that. It shouldn't take that long, even for them." Sarcasm dripped off the split tongue of the Green lizard.

"It could be dangerous." The Group Master turned and looked at the dark lizard squarely. "Our information is incomplete. The species profile on them has never been given a priority. We don't have enough informants to get an accurate understanding of their actions. We have no idea what these creatures are capable of doing or how they will react."

"Is the great Nest of Tri-Bah ancestors suddenly skittish about the scampering of these insignificant animals?"

The Group Master studied the gold snowflake tattoo on the wrist of his marbled green skin and realized just how arrogant this race had become.

"A guest should appreciate his lodgings and the grace of his host." The Group Master didn't feel hospitable or gracious.

"Forgive me, Admiral, if I said anything offensive. I only meant that we have nothing to worry about."

"We have a proverb," the Group Master said, stepping closer. "The scurrying of small animals announces the coming of a large dragon."

Chapter 2

"Namaste, Thomas." The deep rich voice reverberated in English in the small entry alcove. Thomas reached over to a shelf next to the door and picked up and activated his translator. He would need it for anything beyond the greeting. This small alien device of unknown origin was carried by most species.

"Tee, welcome." Thomas recognized the Spike Lizard because he had a cracked rear horn on his right side. The point had been broken off and Tee had not told him how or why. They had met while negotiating a mining contract four years ago, long before his interest in Union politics. But they had kept in touch.

The stillness in the air told Thomas that his guests were nervous. Most humans spent their lives clustered in small holes and didn't come into close contact with intimidating aliens like Tee. Their fears were unjustified but real.

"Forgive me, Thomas, for intruding on your celebration. I wanted to congratulate you on your new position. I know you have worked hard to obtain this social status."

"Thank you, Tee." It always took Thomas a few moments with a translator to get used to the English echo of an alien's speech. "I appreciate your interest." Thomas lowered his voice. "Do you remember what I said about that greeting? Most humans don't appreciate its use by the other species."

"I'm sorry, Thomas, I had forgotten. It seemed most appropriate."

Thomas thought it was appropriate. The guests started to whisper uneasily. He needed to do the polite thing, hopefully, to calm them.

"Everybody, this is Tee, an acquaintance of mine from the time I worked at Brown Brothers Refining. Please have more to eat," he said, forcing a smile.

Charm approached him. "I'll pass out the dessert and get their minds off this."

"Good."

Thomas' association with this ugly lizard had assured him of a level of mutual respect. He had enjoyed their encounters over the years. Every time he saw him with those six horns shooting out of his head, he was reminded of the first joke he had ever heard as a child.

How does a Spike Lizard get into a space suit?
Very carefully.

"Well, Tee, is there something I can get you?"

"No. I will not stay. I wanted to thank you for the suggested reading."

"That's all right. How did you like them?"

"They were all very humorous. Especially the ones by Edgar."

"Edgar?" Armondo asked, as he walked up beside Thomas.

"You mean Poe," Thomas said, clearing the confusion.

"Wait a minute. You think Edgar Allen Poe is funny?"

"Spike Lizard humor is very different." Thomas interjected. Most humans didn't understand those kinds of subtleties. "It's based on the rhyming of words, and not on tragic situations, like ours."

"Even though the translation does not rhyme, I find the original sounds of the words pleasing. In all, an enjoyable study." The lizard focused his stare on Armondo.

"But, what about the content? Don't you find the stories disturbing?" Armondo folded his arms. He had taken a position, preparing himself for a possible difficult discussion. Thomas had seen it many times before from his old friend and been on both sides.

"I thought it a bit ironic."

"Ironic?"

"Please, Armondo, he didn't come here to debate literature." Thomas looked up at Tee's protruding jaw and sharp teeth. "Are you sure I can't get you something? You're not hungry, are you?"

"No. I doubt that you would have anything I would find appetizing. Besides, I must go. I have been called away on other matters. Before I left, I wanted you to know that I appreciated the comic relief." He again lowered his head to get through the door, and out to the hallway of dark stone.

"See'ya later, alligator," Thomas said, knowing their inside joke would please Tee. The simple humor, which translates so well across the two species, would show his acquaintance in a better light to his guest.

Tee stared at Thomas with his burning eyes, "After while, crocodile." He let out a deep rumbling laugh.

Thomas watched as the lizard turned and walked away. A few steps later Tee encountered an elderly couple coming toward him. They let out a silent gasp and backed up to the wall as he went by. The noise returned to the party. The guests were all in a buzz about the tall visitor.

"Can you beat that?" Armondo said, watching the reaction from the old couple. "Do they think they can just go anywhere? Even here on Mitzul."

"It's all right. No harm done. It's the universe we live in. There are stranger and more dangerous creatures among us."

Thomas focused his attention on damage control. Most people could accept the fact that it was all right to deal with them but didn't understand why Tee would be there. Even Thomas found it hard to think of lizards in social situations. Most of the time, when all went well, it was business.

Things were getting back to normal when Charm pulled him aside in the kitchen. He sensed a tamed excitement in her.

"You have a message waiting," she said, with a big smile, "It's Rodriguez."

"What do you suppose he wants?"

"I think he wants to congratulate you on being the Union's newest Representative."

"Do you think so? I never expected that. Well, whatever it is, I shouldn't keep the Director of the Union waiting."

Charm's glowing face beamed back a pride that Thomas loved to see. He would do almost anything to see that look.

"I wish Mark were here to see this."

Thomas also wanted his son to be there. But he was away at school making them both proud.

He went to his small but organized office. The far side wall facing the desk was the only one kept in the original rock surface. The smooth black stone with a gentle diagonal of white marbling had a timeless beauty. All the other walls were covered with fabric or organic textures to make the home, warm and cozy.

Thomas keyed the terminal for the message. The image of a face with rugged hard lines under a short gray beard appeared. He was the man considered to be the most powerful human.

"Director, it's so good to see you again."

"Thomas, I'm going to get right to the point. We don't have a lot of time."

Caught off guard, Thomas expected a friendlier and more casual conversation, but Rodriguez had something on his mind.

"My information shows me you have relatives on Bohica?"

"Yes, my wife's sister is a surveyor. In fact, she is marrying one of the youngest chief mining engineers in the sector. We're very happy for her and looking forward to visiting them. Perhaps sometime next year after the Union session is over."

"Thomas." The word snapped.

"Yes, I'm sorry. Please go on," he said, feeling like a talkative child.

"There has been an incident at Bohica. We have no idea what is going on. The Q-space com relays are open and functioning, but we can't communicate."

"Wait a minute, what kind of incident?"

"In the last message, they mentioned some ships arriving. It might have been some hostile action against the Bohica colony. Then again, maybe nothing."

"What do you mean, hostile?"

"Thomas, I need you to go there, immediately, in an official capacity. Report to me, what has happened."

"Now? Why me?"

"You are at the far edge of our influence and the closest Rep. You can get there sooner than anyone else. Besides, I understand you were part of the original team that negotiated the rights to Bohica."

"That was a long time ago, and only during the beginning of the talks. Look. I'm not ready for this. I haven't even been sworn in yet. The ceremony isn't for another three days. The Governor is going to preside. It's very important to all of us here." This was happening too fast, and Thomas didn't feel the need for urgency.

"I have already talked with the governor, and smoothed things out with him. I can't make you go, but I need you to be there." Rodriguez's face looked grim, and the hard lines deepened, "You might want to consider the political implication if you refuse."

Thomas wasn't sure what that meant, but it didn't sound encouraging. Turning down this challenge could label him. A *can't do* kind of guy to the other Representatives. It would be harder to get assigned to any of the good project rosters.

"There must be some ship in the area close by that, could drop in, and say hello?"

"Thomas, we need a Rep who can be trusted. You have a background in negotiations and dealing with aliens. You have a vested interest in the well-being of Bohica. You're the ideal person. Now, stop wasting my time. Are you going or not?" Rodriguez let silence continue his argument.

"Yes, I'll go." He said, not believing his words. He didn't want to take a trip right now, but it did make sense. Refusing such a simple request seemed ridiculous.

A smile formed behind the gray fuzzy beard and Rodriguez's eyes softened.

"I'm sending you all the information we have. Personally, I don't think it's the Fire Lizards. That wouldn't make any sense. My hunch is that Commodore Black has opened up his illegal operations and is getting bolder."

"Who?"

"Ivan Black. The latest information I have has him working in that sector. You must be cautious. He's a suspected marauder and has the resources to make a move on a small colony like Bohica.

"Your shuttle leaves in one hour. Your Community Clerk will meet you there to swear you in as a Representative to the Union. A title, I might add, I have never taken lightly. We have contracted with a survey ship, the *Gold Rat*, to take you to Bohica, and investigate the conditions as found. You can render immediate emergency aid if necessary. But don't try to get involved with any hostile forces. Do I make myself clear?"

"Yes," Thomas said with reluctance. He wasn't sure he could do that. If the colony is under attack, he would want to help. That would only be human.

"Make your reports directly to me and under no circumstances tell anyone anything about what you are doing."

"But, what about . . . "

"Good luck, Thomas. The Union is counting on you." Rodriguez's face disappeared from the screen.

Thomas stared at the blank terminal. The many unanswered questions in his mind slowly gave way to a sinking fear. If he got into trouble at Bohica, the Union couldn't do anything to help. They had no navy or troops to speak of. A few planetary patrols and hired escort ships were all the treasury could afford. The Union had always been a place where humans could work out their problems with each other and provide unified representation for mankind. It couldn't defend a planet against major opposition. Maybe it could fend off a few marauders, but it would be too late. Bohica might have already been ransacked.

As he transferred a record of the conversation and the information Rodriguez had sent to a media chip, Thomas's thoughts raced. He plucked the tiny cube from the small drawer on the side of the terminal. Lists of all his tasks, and appointments to cancel from that short conversation went through his head. He had worked for weeks preparing for the trip to take Charm and himself to his new job. Now he found himself going in the opposite direction.

He wondered what the first day on his new job would be like a waste of time, a wild chase to nowhere or maybe a total disaster? With less than an hour before leaving, he squelched his fears.

Telling Charm, he had to leave would be easier than explaining why. She would see through any kind of a lie. All his attempts in the past of trying to keep a secret or to surprise her inevitably failed. And the truth had a simplicity he could live with. She walked in on him as he was rummaging through the closet.

"What's going on," she asked? "Did you talk with Rodriguez?"

"Have you seen my space shoes?"

"They're in the hall storage. What are you doing?"

Thomas did his best to explain. "There are no communications from Bohica. Some kind of incident or accident has occurred. We're not sure." Thomas had to stand there and watch her face change.

"No," she said, quietly, painfully.

"Rodriguez has asked me to go there and investigate what happened."

"Please find out if Angelica is all right."

"I'll do whatever I can. You know that. But I'm sure everything is fine. I'm sure it's just a com glitch," he said with all the reassurance he could muster. "I'll just be running around for a couple of weeks."

If there were real problems out there, Thomas wasn't sure he could do anything except, file the report. Hopefully a short one.

"It's a shame it has to be now with all of our plans."

"I know. Please go tell our guests I've been called away on an emergency business trip and will be back in a few weeks."

She started to go, then turned back, and put her arms around him. "Please be careful."

Holding her tight, he nestled his face in her hair, breathed in her fragrance and hoped its memory would linger with him until he returned. He hated going on business trips alone.

He changed his clothes to something more suitable for traveling. Fortunately, Charm had taught him how to pack a small bag, keeping things to a minimum and still having all he needed. While over by the chest, he caught himself in the mirror. Should he let his beard grow in, a common practice when dealing with aliens? Apparently, it made humans less threatening, and more universally mammalian-looking in appearance. But they might not be dealing with other species. It had been a while since the last time he grew one and he didn't want to know how much lighter in color his beard had turned. There was enough grey around the edges of his dark hair already. He decided to stay as human as possible.

Thomas picked up his knife to put it on, the same one he had worn at the party. The blade Charm gave him years ago looked beautiful, ornate and quite suitable for the new direction in his life of formality and protocol. But it wasn't right for a non-ceremonial trip. He opened the narrow stone box sitting on the chest. It held other blades from his family. His great grandfather's, his grandfather's and the knife his father had given him when he became old enough to have a real blade. He had worn the classic Kanashimi proudly for more than twenty-five years. This style was often worn by the more idealistic and passionate about traditions. Good friends were hard to leave behind. He removed the old silvery knife from the sheath.

Nothing could remind him more of the importance of his family: past, present and future.

"I will find out what happened at Bohica and see that Angelica is safe. I make that promise," he said, and on the flat just above the hilt he kissed the blade.

His commitment clear, he sheathed the knife, attached it to the loops on the side of his pants and left for his appointment.

The hectic ride in the shuttle up to space left the clerk as rattled as Thomas. He asked Thomas questions and recorded his responses. The questions were the same as he had rehearsed. But instead of giving the answers he had been carefully writing for the ceremony, he just said yes or no. They finished as the shuttle docked with the *Gold Rat.*

The clerk shook Thomas's hand. "Congratulations, Thomas McCormick for being the elected Representative of the planet Mitzul to the Union of Humanity. Good luck, sir."

"Thank you." Thomas got his bag out of the storage compartment. As the air lock opened, an attractive woman with short red hair stepped through, took the luggage from his hand and disappeared back through the hatch. He followed.

As he moved onto the other ship, both airlock doors closed behind him. After securing the hatch, the woman turned and left. Thomas felt a shift in the deck as the two crafts separated. He started to make his way out of the small compartment when the ship lunged. He flew backwards against the deck. His feet went up, and his head down. Pain shot through his skull.

*   *   *

Victor, the rag trader, could see Armondo quickly approaching his cubicle. Light tan tapestry of the walls defined his area of doing business. The rag trader hated to meet with this informant.

In the dimly lit expanse people were talking, tinkering out jewelry, fashioning crafts and trading junk. The high ceiling of the cavern blended the individual sounds into a thunderous noise.

"You're late," he said, looking at Armondo through squinting eyes. He sat on a worn rug covering the stone floor, surrounded by neat piles of used cloth.

"I'm not given the same freedom to come and go as you. I must be careful."

"All right. What news?"

"Something unusual has happened. Thomas has been called away. He walked out of his party and left."

"That's not strange enough to bring you down here to rub noses with a weasel. You've got to do better than that. Where did he go?"

"Don't know."

"What did his wife say?"

"Charm was not much help. She gave me the polite runaround she gave everyone else." Armondo looked hurt.

Victor didn't care about the feelings of his sources, especially the ones that had better lives than he did, and that was most of them.

"So, what did she say, exactly?"

"You know the kinds of stuff people like that say. She said he was urgently called away on unexpected business. She thanked us all and said that they would see us another time. Then we were hustled out the door. But there are two things that you might think are suspicious."

"Go on."

"Thomas received a message from the Director, then bolted for a shuttle, off planet."

"Well, why didn't you say so? What could that lizard lover be up to?" Victor asked, rubbing the stubby whiskers on his chin and turning his head to the canvas partition. "Why did he leave? It wouldn't be official business. He's not a Rep yet."

"Perhaps it's personal or an old business contact." Armondo leaned closer.

"You told me he hasn't seen any of his contacts since he started this whole Union nonsense, a year-and-a-half ago. But you could be right about something personal. But why would the Director be involved? What's the other bit of news?"

"A spike lizard came during the party."

"What did they talk about?" The rag trader became more attentive and stared into Armondo's face.

"Poetry, according to Thomas, if you believe that."

"Poetry?" He lowered his head into his hands and rubbed his temples. "Go back to Thomas's apartment."

"Why? What good would that do? He's gone."

"Go and find out more. You've brought too little."

"I'm not sure I can get any more."

"Just go. Go lay bright your day." His hands waved for him to leave.

Armondo got up and disappeared into the crowd.

Thomas McCormick had turned into a poor hunch. Armondo's devotion to Thomas had gotten in the way for the last time. He should forget about both of them. If there were any useful information to learn, he would have to find another informant, but not Armondo.

And why should he waste time on this impotent Union Rep? Victor couldn't explain it, but he knew. Because of the odd feeling that wouldn't shake loose. Yes, and a strange sense of quiet, as if there will be a storm.

Chapter 3

"Namaste, Mr. McCormick, my name is Lee-Hope, and I'll be your purser during your stay on the *Gold Rat*," a smiling child said. She wore long red braids and looks about ten or eleven. As she extended her hand to help Thomas up off the deck, he saw an adult-size blade at her side.

"I'm sorry about that. My dad is in a hurry. We made the jump as soon as you got on board."

"That's all right. It just took me by surprise." Thomas rubbed a sore spot behind his ear. "I'd forgotten how hard that first bump can be, especially when it's on your head."

"Do you require medical attention? We have a well-stocked first aid kit."

"No. That's all right. I'll be fine."

"This way," she said, turning down the narrow corridor.

He followed. They passed an Escape Pod entrance and went up a flight of stairs to emerge into the large compartment. Thomas' traveling experience told him it looked typical for a ship its size. An oval table with a curved bench built into the wall that occupied one side. On the other, a food work area with storage and prep dominated the space. The lady he had glimpsed earlier greeted him.

"I'm Taffa-Lee, Survey Officer and Co-captain of the *Gold Rat*. My husband, Ned, is Pilot and Co-captain. He's kind of busy right now, and so am I. Lee-Hope will show you to your compartment and see to your needs. She can answer any questions about accommodations."

"Are we headed to Bohica?"

"Yes," she said, and turned and ascended another set of stairs.

"I'll show you the cabin," Lee-Hope said.

For paying passengers they also had two coffin cabins, one on top of the other. Next to them, was a walk-in closet for Thomas.

"This is the Presidential Cubby," Lee-Hope said, extending her arm, and grinning from braid to braid.

"Looks cozy."

"We can sleep up to ten comfortably."

Space was always at a premium on a small ship. Extraordinary measures were often taken to achieve efficiency. Still, he gave her a disbelieving glance.

"Well, friendly people."

Two could stand in the room, if they were embracing. The top bunk contained boxes, netted to prevent movement. Thomas put his bag on the bottom bunk. The middle one also served as a chair with a ledge big enough for a few personal things. He sat on the surprisingly comfortable bed, probably due to the slightly lower gravity.

"If you need anything or have questions, push this button. We'll do whatever we can to make your stay comfortable," she said before disappearing.

Thomas decided to scan the information Rodriguez had sent and see if there were anything revealing he should know. He needed to feed his ignorance. Placing his terminal on the ledge, he reviewed his previous communication with the Director. He couldn't believe how stupid he'd acted during his conversation with his new superior. He must have looked like an idiot. Maybe he would be given the job of court jester on Ichorous. Perhaps succeeding at this task would put him in a better light. Yes, but he didn't need the pressure to do well.

There were two knocks outside of his compartment and the door opened. A tall man stepped in and glared down at him.

"Where is the escort we were promised?"

Thomas tried to stand, but the crowded closeness made it difficult. This, along with the surprise of the intrusion, caused him to lose his balance. He sat back down awkwardly and looked up.

"The Union contact said we would have a small Dagger and a Defender class ship to accompany us when we arrive at Bohica. The *Monkey's Fist* jumped with us at Mitzul. Now where is the other ship? We contracted this job with two escorts for a good reason. I'm not jeopardizing this ship and the people in it on a potentially dangerous job without someone to cover the rear. Do you understand?"

Thomas succeeded at his second attempt to rise. The man in the compartment backed up to the entranceway. He had close-cropped dark hair and beard. His eyes showed he was sincerely upset. Thomas hoped that his outburst would help defuse the situation by giving him a chance to vent whatever frustrations he held.

"You must be Ned," he said, sticking out his hand, "I'm Thomas."

"Where's the ship?" Ned asked.

"I don't know."

"Well, then, I'm turning around. There's no point in doing this if you're not going to meet the contract," he said, disappearing from view into the passageway.

"Wait," Thomas followed him, "give me a chance to look over the contract, and the other information I have. I'm still not completely informed."

Ned stopped and gave him a puzzled look.

"I thought you were the expert on this situation."

"I just found out."

"How long will it take?"

"A few hours, maybe," Thomas' mind raced.

"You'll have all the answers by then?"

"Not all, but maybe enough to decide if we should go on or not."

"Okay, two hours." Ned held up two fingers to emphasize the point.

Back in his cubby, Thomas reviewed the information he'd hoped would have the answers. It became obvious that he knew nothing about what had really happened. But then nobody did, as the alarming shortage of facts showed. He now saw the importance of going to Bohica and seeing the situation firsthand. However, Thomas questioned, if he should be the person doing this?

As lavish as his room had been outfitted, it lacked one necessity. He pushed the button to buzz Lee-Hope. Unlike her father, she knocked, and waited for a response before entering.

"What can I do for you, Mr. McCormick?" she asked.

"I need to use the lavatory. Where is it?"

"Down here the third door on the right. The sanitary room is next to it, with your time schedule posted on the door."

When he returned, he found Lee-Hope still in his cubby, sitting on the middle bunk, swinging her legs, humming to herself. Thomas sat in front of his terminal.

"I got some new scrunches," she said, showing him an open hand with colorful bits of metal in interesting shapes.

Picking up a triangle, he could tell they were stained titanium with a clip on one side--the material of common costume jewelry. She had two others at the ends of her braids.

"They're very pretty."

"Thank you. We were surveying asteroids in the secondary ring of the Qu Patch system for the Landerians. Have you ever seen a Landerian? They are so strange."

"Lee-Hope, I need to get back to this."

"But they smell good."

"Your father really wants me to put some stuff together for him."

"I know. I'll leave you alone."

"I'm sure we'll have plenty of time to talk later."

"Okay, later," she said, pointing a finger at him and making a clicking sound with her tongue to punctuate the movement. She reminded him of his son at that age--into everything, and afraid of nothing.

As he read the contract, it seemed to be a very simple and open-ended agreement. Another ship would join them. The *Gold Rat* would do whatever the Union, or its representatives, felt necessary to investigate and verify the stability of Bohica. Lend any assistance, if necessary. The risk levels were very well laid out.

He hoped there would be more information about the incident itself. But most of the communication logs given to him just confirmed what little he knew. Four ships of an unknown configuration had appeared from Q-space. The ships moved toward the planet, communication stopped, the Q-space com links and frogging repeaters were all working. They've heard nothing since. Not quite your normal day.

Hijacker, marauder, and pirate activities were at a minimum in that area. The closest alien presence was the Tri-Bah or Fire Lizards, but humans negotiated Bohica from them. It seemed unlikely they would want it back so soon. They would at least wait until Bohica had become a rich producer, and then demand it back. He had seen that before. Perhaps a new player had moved into the area. If so, the Fire Lizards might turn into reluctant allies.

It hadn't felt like two hours, but Lee-Hope knocked, and stuck her head into his cubby. "My dad says we're ready for you now in Operations."

Thomas grabbed his terminal and made his way forward. Again, he thought about the importance of doing this simple task. If anyone had any doubts, he had to convince them otherwise, and not just for his career. He didn't think he could face Charm with the fate of her sister still in doubt. Besides, he'd made a promise.

He entered from stairs into the business area of the ship. The walls were a natural green and the floor a light brown. This was common for a small ship. Everyone looked at him from the central table. Besides Lee-Hope and her mother and father, there were two others. Ned stood up to make introductions.

"This is Rusty, our Sensory Engineer, and his wife Martha-Key, our statistician. She does our analysis." Rusty extended a meaty hand. He had a warm smile, through a full light-colored beard. Martha-Key gave him a cold nod. Thomas thought it was sweet that Rusty and Martha-Key wore matching blades. He sat at the only open place left. Ned seemed much calmer, and Thomas hoped easier to deal with.

"This is a copy of everything I have about the incident at Bohica. And I want you to understand that I'm keeping nothing from you. I feel it's important to have a mutual trust," he said, taking a media chip and laying it on the table.

"Where's the other ship?" Ned was at least consistent.

"The *Assegai* will meet us there. It's a defender class ship and should arrive shortly after we do."

They all looked disappointed.

"Is there a problem with that?"

"Yes. We are most vulnerable right after popping into a system. That's when we need the most protection."

"I'm sorry. I didn't make the arrangements."

"That's all right. We'll deal with it. But, if there is anything that looks hostile or doesn't meet the agreement, we're out of there."

"I understand and wouldn't blame you."

"Fine. Do you have any questions for us?" Ned leaned forward, and put his elbows on the table, looking more relaxed.

"Yes, I do have a few," Thomas said, relieved that at least one hurdle had been passed. "How soon will we get there?" Everyone's attention turned to Rusty.

"What do the latest calculations make our speed?" Taffa-Lee asked.

"Well, the instruments say we're doing a virtual speed of about forty-two Puffs, so we should be there in. . . . Let's say ninety standard hours," Rusty said, stroking his beard.

"What's a Puff?" Thomas asked. He hadn't heard that term before.

"P P F, is Parsecs Per Fortnight."

"You must excuse Rusty. He's an old, retired Quantum Metrologist. Sometimes he thinks in different terms, just to make it difficult," Martha-Key added.

"To make it fun and exercise the mind that's all."

"One of the things I'm interested in is exactly what will happen when we get there," Thomas continued.

"We're not sure," Ned replied, "but what we're going to do is standard for this type of survey. As soon as we pop into the system, we'll scan it for other ships. The best place to do that is above or below the planetary plane. It will make it harder for any hostile to hide. After we feel the system is safe, we'll concentrate on Bohica. Primary importance would be to establish communication, and to survey for any damage. If needed, we'll render assistance. Filling out a report, or submitting the findings is your responsibility. We will provide all of the reading and data we take during the survey to back up your report."

"That sounds good, but what if there are hostile, as you call them. What happens then?"

"We'd have to decide who they are and how large their group is before jumping."

"Are you saying that you wouldn't try to help?" Thomas asked this question not thinking of the contract, but instead remembering the last time he saw Angelica and Charm together. They had such a wonderful time laughing and giggling like school children.

"Look, Thomas," Ned leaned closer, "we are not an armed ship. It's our duty to report what we find so others can take up where we leave off. However, what the *Monkey's Fist* does after we're safely gone is up to them. Can you accept that?"

"Yes," Thomas replied. What could he be thinking? Of course, they couldn't do anything. They didn't even have a rock to throw. Unfortunately, they were a long way from help if Bohica needed it.

"Are there any other questions you have for us?"

"No, not until I know more."

"Good. It's time to seal the deal," Taffa-Lee said, as she and Rusty got up from the table.

"O-boy, I love this part," Lee-Hope said, breaking her well-behaved silence.

"What part?" Thomas asked.

"You see, Thomas," Ned said, leaning back crossing his arms, "we like to have our employers that travel with us consummate the agreement in traditional *Gold Rat* fashion."

Rusty reappeared and placed a large pot in the center of the table. A strange and pungent aroma hit Thomas' senses.

"Rusty's black bean chili." Lee-Hope looked at Thomas with a toothy smile.

Bowls and spoons were produced as Ned continued.

"Earlier, you talked of trust. We feel that taking food from a common pot is an expression of good faith. In the past some of our hairier and scalier bosses have declined."

"It's really hard to give a hundred-percent to someone who doesn't like Rusty's chili," Martha-Key added. It sounded like a challenge.

"Smells, good!" Thomas added a hint of the truth to an exaggeration.

CHAPTER 4

"Namaste," the middle-aged overweight man with a brown and gray beard said. "Are you Victor?"

"Yes. And you are?"

"We talked earlier. I'm the shuttle pilot. Just call me Phil."

"Good. Follow me," the rag trader said, moving down the main corridor leading to an empty utility hanger. Most of the shuttle departures and much of the small cargo went through here before leaving Mitzul. Weaving through the traffic of people and lorries carrying crates, they made their way through the caves to a dimly lit alcove and sat at a bench cut from the stone walls.

The day had been busy for Victor following up on the information Armondo had given him. He felt like it had turned into another waste of time. His frustration level had moved close to overload.

Thomas McCormick probably had a small family emergency off-planet somewhere and it should be forgotten. But he couldn't let it go. Uneasiness stirred in his chest.

"Phil, I understand that you took a passenger up yesterday, by the name of McCormick."

"That's correct, the new Representative. I didn't vote for him. He and this other man went up together. A clerk, I believe. He came back with me."

"Did you hear any of the conversation?"

"You know, Victor, I remember someone saying that our talk would be rewarding."

"That's true." Victor reluctantly reached into a breast pocket and removed a small envelope.

"That's more like it." Phil felt the slight bulge of the content and smiled. "He swore Mr. McCormick in as a Representative. You know, I always voted against that Union crap. It's not like we don't have enough people trying to tell us what to do."

"Thomas is a rep?" This changed the possibilities. New scenarios ran through Victor's mind. He caught himself just looking off into nowhere. "Please, Phil, continue."

"We hooked up with a survey rig, the *Gold Rat*. Then they left, along with another ship. We were docked for only a few seconds. They were in a hurry to scoot."

"What was the nature of the other ship?"

"An escort. Saber class, I believe. I wasn't told the name."

"So, they seemed to be in a hurry?" As Victor asked the question, he wondered why they needed protection?

"Oh, yeah. They jumped right in front of me. That's very rude from one pilot to another."

"Do you know where they were going?"

"Maybe. It's not like they said. But I'm a naturally curious fellow. Especially since the Union arranged the whole deal." Phil displayed a smug grin.

"Okay, where did they go?"

"I recorded their Q-space vectors as they jumped."

"Yes, where were they headed?"

"It seems like that bit of information might be worth a little more than you've given me here. You know, above and beyond what we discussed."

"No. We agreed on a fair price for all you had," Victor said, controlling his temper.

"I don't see it that way," the shuttle pilot said, as he stood up to leave. "You think about it and contact me when you're ready to deal."

The pilot's smile turned into a full grin, and he started to walk away.

Victor could not take yet another frustrating dead-end. Events of the last thirty-six hours had ground his courtesy to nothing. He jumped up, grabbed the man's collar, and put the shuttle pilot back in his seat. A surprised expression looked up from the pilot as Victor removed his knife and held it to the bearded face of the larger man.

For a sixty-five-year-old rag trader, he couldn't believe what he had done. It took all his effort to keep his hand steady.

"We're not bankers arguing over the price of rocks. Tell me what I need to know, or I'll separate your tongue from the rest of you. Where did they go?"

The eyes of the larger man grew wide with genuine fear. Victor was not about to back down at this point.

"They're on their way to sector TT42 or 43. I couldn't get any closer without following them."

"That would be either Hector, Bohica, or Fallen."

"You know the area pretty well."

"You said the Union arranged all of this?"

"Yeah, the Alien Relations Project took care of everything. They arranged for my shuttle and the other three ships."

"You only mentioned two." Victor's hand relaxed its grip on Phil's collar.

"The other ship is an escort diverted from the evacuation on Tuska."

"But why there? And why would they need a survey ship?"

"Oh, you mean that sector?" The pilot seemed very cooperative.

"Yes. Why TT42?"

"Well, the rumor from the ship captains around here is that Bohica has gone quiet. Maybe it's nothing, but it could be marauders or those damn lizards again. A survey rig would come in handy if you were checking for damage or mounting a rescue. That's all I know, honest."

"I'm sorry about the knife Phil, but this is very important."

"I understand."

"Thanks, you've been most helpful."

"Sure," Phil said, looking puzzled.

The stirring in Victor's chest sank to his stomach as he moved away as fast as he dared without making a scene. He couldn't believe he had pulled a knife on another human. By the time he'd made it through the passageways and down the many levels to his small quarters, he was shaking.

Turning on the small light over his narrow pallet, he sank to his knees. He removed the frayed cloth from the top of an old crate and lifted the hinged lid. Carefully removing the book, he clenched it to his chest, bowed his head, and inhaled the musty fragrance of the yellowed pages.

Tzu would soon talk to him, comfort him, and clear his vision, but not just yet. For his terrible actions against a fellow human a price would be paid. He would allow the contempt, shame and fear to wash over and soak him to the bone, but only for a little while to remind him that he was also human. Then his strength would return. He felt his time was close at hand.

*   *   *

Thomas quickly recovered from the side effects of the chili. By the time his insides had settled down, he felt a greater acceptance from the crew.

He spent his time resting, catching up on his growing correspondence and reviewing information about the operation on Bohica. A couple of times, during to trip, he helped Lee-Hope with her schoolwork. Martha-Key also served as tutor on the ship, and surprisingly, she encouraged Thomas' assistance. She wanted Lee-Hope to get as many views and opinions as possible because of her lack of contact with other people.

Thomas wasn't very good with the math and the technical subjects, but he could help with the history and language. They sat at the table in the operations area and studied the terminal.

"So, it means the same as Namaste?" Lee-Hope asked.

"No, not exactly. Aloha is both hello and goodbye. It comes from the most incredibly beautiful place that some have defined as paradise. The word conveys a certain optimism. But after the Kanashimi, the term became unpopular during the sorrow that followed."

"Why?"

"It then stood for paradise lost."

"Well, what does Namaste mean?"

"It's also a greeting that says there is a place inside of you where the whole universe exists."

"That's a big place."

"Yes, it is. But it also means that the same place lives in me, because I'm also human. If you are at peace with that place in you and I'm at peace with that place in me, then we are at peace with each other."

"That's nice."

"Yes, it is. Humans have found comfort in sharing that thought with each other."

"Is the place where Aloha came from still beautiful?"

"No. It's no longer there."

He enjoyed the time with Lee-Hope. Again, it reminded him of the many hours he had spent with his own son. It wouldn't be long before Lee-Hope would be a teenager and more difficult to contain.

When it came time to enter Bohicas' system, everyone had something specific to do except Thomas. He had to dissipate his nervousness by standing and watching over their shoulders in the operations area. Even Lee-Hope had her station, keeping the systems warmed up in the escape pod. Thomas wished he could be with her.

"Approaching the interface," Ned's voice said calmly. He sat above in the pilot's chair.

The *Gold Rat* jolted violently for just an instant as the alarm sounded. Thomas hung onto a table. The rough transition stopped.

"That's worse than normal," Rusty said, looking up from his console.

Next to him sat Taffa-Lee. "Let's take a quick look around. Make sure everything is okay."

"I don't see Bohica," Rusty said.

"What do you mean?" Thomas asked, his curiosity moving him closer to Rusty's station.

"There's another ship in the area," Martha-Key said.

"It's not showing up." Rusty played with the settings on the terminal.

"The *Monkey's Fist* is maneuvering between us and the unknown ship. Rusty, can you detect any transponder codes from that ship?" Taffa-Lee said.

"This could be the wrong system," Thomas interjected.

"This is the *Gold Rat*, please identify yourselves," Martha-Key said. She also did the communication.

"Not unless we were given the wrong information," Rusty's voice cracked.

"Its power system jumped to the rail. Its weapons are armed," Taffa-Lee yelled.

"Rusty, would you check it again," Ned asked.

"Ned are you ready to get us out of here?" shouted, Taffa-Lee.

"It's not here," Rusty said.

"They're tracking us." Martha-Key's voice squawked.

"What are you talking about?" Taffa-Lee turned and glared at Rusty. "It's got to be there."

"This is the *Gold Rat*, identify yourselves."

Thomas felt helpless and lost. He was going to die in the wrong place.

CHAPTER 5

"Namaste." Victor had only one decent contact on Ichorous, and her face stared back at him from the terminal. He could have researched someone else from other operatives but that would have taken time. It had been more than two years since he had talked with Penelope-Vu. Her information had always proved fair but came at a price. Her mind games became more than Victor could take. But today he was desperate.

"Penelope-Vu, how are you?" He loved saying that to put her on the defensive.

"Cut the crap. You little weasel. What do you want?"

"I've been hearing some disturbing rumors, and I knew I could count on you to straighten everything out for me."

"What makes you think I'll help you? I told you the last time, which you still owe me for, I won't have anything to do with you. Do you know the danger it puts me in?"

"Danger? Are you kidding me? This is for a very good cause."

"You always say that, but I've got refugees up to my eyeballs from Tuska to deal with. Unless you want to help? Is there room at your place for, let's say, a hundred families?"

"You know I have nothing to do with that situation."

"Then what good are you?" She said.

"Please, Penelope, tell me what I can help with." Victor hoped she couldn't see through his veneer.

She ran the fingers of both hands through her short blond hair and took a deep breath. "All right, what do you want?"

"Talk to me about sector TT42; what are our lizard friends up to?"

"How do you know . . .?" She stopped. Her face became serious. "Don't cling to any illusions, Victor, you can't help. No one can. It's all over."

"So, it's true."

"I didn't say that," she said. "Just go back to your own petty intrigues and forget it. This is over your head. With any luck, Rodriguez will smooth it all out, and keep the impact to a minimum."

"You've worked for him too long." Victor could hear the sarcasm in his words. "Rodriguez's toothless diplomacy is worthless. He has nothing and the flimsy support he could muster would be pathetic. It will take much more."

"Victor, what are you talking about?"

"Forget it. Tell me who's responsible."

"You know I can't do that."

"Yes, you can. I won't let you use that ploy." Victor's Impatience came through his voice. "Was it the Tri-Bah or the Keet?"

"I can't say. We're not sure. That's the truth, Victor."

"Then who do you think it is?" Victor stared at the short haired blond woman and wished his talk was over.

"Well, it sure wasn't the Keet. If you're smart, Victor, you'll forget all this and go back to your market."

"I'm not that smart. I must go. Goodbye, and thank you, Penelope-Vu."

He reached over and disconnected the link at the terminal. With her defeated face gone he felt tired and thought about rest. No, he could sleep when he was dead. The promise of a busy night lay before him.

*　　*　　*

"Namaste, *Gold Rat* and *Monkey's Fist*." A beautiful dark face with short black hair appeared in the corner of the console.

"Safrona-Lu, it's been a long time," Martha-Key answered. "I thought you were going to join us a little later?"

"We made good time and arrived about an hour ago. Then you showed up and gave us quite a scare."

"How could we frighten you? You're twice as big as the two of us put together."

"We were only expecting one ship."

Taffa-Lee and Ted shot Thomas a harsh look. Even though he had no control over the situation, he would be responsible for the screw-up. After all, he represented the Union.

"It's good to see you, and know that you're here," Taffa-Lee said. "We've got a lot of work to do, and I don't want to stick around here any longer than we have to. Let's get started."

"Hey, Safrona-Lu," Rusty cut in, "what did you do with Bohica?"

"I was about to ask you the same thing."

"What do you mean?" Taffa-Lee asked Rusty.

"Did we take a wrong turn?" Thomas said, then everyone looked at him. "What?"

"This system doesn't have a planet where Bohica should be. This is preliminary, but it looks all wrong."

"Ned, are we in the right place?" Taffa-Lee looked angry.

"Just a minute, I'm playing back the navigation log." Ned studied the terminal then said, "Yes, it's the same route we used three years ago when we were here. This is the place."

"What's the confidence on your readings, Ned?" Martha-Key asked.

"What do you mean, my readings? I'm telling you what it is."

"That's enough," Taffa-Lee's stern voice seemed to quiet everyone.

Thomas could tell they were frightened, but Taffa-Lee's face expressed it best.

She took a moment, then looked at her husband. "Ned, would you take us to a point where we can get a clear scan of the whole system?" She then returned her attention to the console. "Safrona-Lu, have the *Assegai* take up a cavalry Position. *Monkey Fist*, you stay with us."

After that, everyone seemed to know what needed to be done and went to work. All except Thomas. He had no more or less to do than before, he could only watch.

Five hours later everyone on the *Gold Rat* sat around the table eating a quickly prepared meal and going over the findings. Primarily for Thomas' benefit, the findings had the group in a somber mood.

"The good news is that we are in the right system," Rusty sounded tired. "The sun signature is correct. The outer planet moon count is right on the mark, and distances between objects are well within norm."

"Then what is the problem?" Thomas could sense a reluctance in their faces. He had seen it before as a negotiator, when the other party wasn't willing to give up the prize or secret. But why would they hide anything?

"This system should have seven planets. It only has six. Bohica is missing."

"Well, where is it?"

"We don't know. The planetary mass distribution says one should be here." Rusty pointed to the terminal in the center of the table. "Right between the second and third planets is a gap. It's a hole that should be filled with Bohica."

"Where is it?"

"Look, Mr. McCormick," Ned leaned forward, "we don't know."

Thomas felt a cold distance in his voice. It held more than just fear. They hadn't used 'Mr.' since they ate the black bean chili. A change had taken place. Had he turned into a snake? "All right, what's going on?"

"We really don't know what happened to Bohica."

"I'm not talking about that. What's happening here? Do you not trust me, are you scared, are we in danger? Is there something you're not telling me?"

As the silence stretched out, Thomas realized that even Lee-Hope looked sad.

"We feel that we have done our job, and our work is finished," Taffa-Lee said. "We feel we should leave."

"If it's payment you're worried about, I'm authorized to take care of that."

"It's not money."

"What is it?"

"We can't do a survey on something that isn't here. We're leaving. All of us have other commitments, and the *Assegai* wants to get back to Tuska to help with the evacuation," Taffa-Lee lowered her eyes.

"There's more going on here than just an obligation to some job. More than two thousand people were on that planet. We owe it to them and their families to find out what happened. We don't even know if they're alive." Thomas found himself angry. How could they leave?

"I understand how you must feel."

"No, I don't think you do. Maybe it's because I know someone on the planet. My wife's sister is a dear member of my family, but it's more than that. Those people. . .." Thomas said, standing up from the table. "Those humans are also members of our family. They have gotten a rotten deal from every other species their whole life. All they have is what we have--each other. We must learn if they are safe."

"We're sorry, Thomas, we've made our decision," Ned told him.

"If you leave, I'll just find another ship and come back. I must find out their fate." Thomas turned away and took the half dozen steps to the stairs leading down to his cabin.

As he hesitated at the stairs, he glanced back. Their silence shattered his hope of changing their minds. He felt foolish but needed to make his report to Rodriguez and see what could be done to get another ship. He realized the Union might not want to pursue the investigation. What would happen to his career if he ignored them and did it on his own? And what would he say to Charm?

Out of the corner of his eye, he saw Lee-Hope do an odd thing. She removed her knife from its sheath attached at her thigh and placed it on the table. He descended the stairs to his cabin thinking about what to say to the Director.

*　　*　　*

A short high-pitched squeal sounded. The Tri-Bah Group Master sat on pillows at his desk and pulled himself upright. Doing this would be unnecessary for an officer in his own command. That arrogant Green lizard had an unknown agenda the Group Master couldn't trust. It required the maximum commanding presence.

Group Master quickly covered some information sensitive areas on his desk and hit the release button for the door. His Group

Commander and the green marbled lizard entered and stood in front of the low desk.

"We've just received a communication from *Rock-five*, on patrol near the demonstration sight," the Group Master said.

"Are the animals there?" The Green lizard asked as his eyes widened.

"Yes. They have arrived."

"Good."

"We will see how intelligent these creatures are. Group Commander, keep them on station and monitor the system. Inform me of their movements. That's all."

The Group Commander turned for the door but the Green lizard didn't move.

"When will we interact with them?" He asked.

"I hope we won't have to. Why should we scare the animals any more than needed?" The Group Master wanted him to just leave.

"I was hoping to learn more through direct observation."

"We will see," the Group Master turned his attention to the work on his desk. The Green lizard finally left.

CHAPTER 6

"Namaste, Director, it's good to see you again." Thomas lowered his head to his hands. "No, no, I can't say that." He fought to get up the courage to contact Rodriguez. He didn't feel at one with the universe or people or at peace with anything. Practicing in front of a blank terminal didn't make it any better. The small dim cabin gave him no comfort. It felt like a tomb. A knock came from the door.

"Yes."

"Excuse me, Mr. McCormick, may I come in?" Taffa-Lee asked. She sat next to him.

"What is it?"

"We have reconsidered your argument and have decided to stay. We will begin looking for Bohica at first watch. We're all a little tired right now."

Thomas couldn't believe what she said. "Why did you change your mind?" Maybe he would do better making grand speeches at the Union than he thought. Had he really changed the situation?

"We were all very close to that decision and you were right about the responsibility to the people concerned." She gave him a small smile.

"Thank you," he said. Her expression looked like an apology to Thomas. At least he took it that way. "What about the other ships?"

"They're also staying."

"Good. I can put off sending my message to Rodriguez," he said, feeling relieved.

"Don't you find it odd talking directly with him and not going through some committee or branch of the Union?"

"What do you mean?"

"We were all contacted by the Alien Relations Project."

"I'm sure it's just to keep the information quiet, so the situation doesn't get out of hand," Thomas said, but he didn't like the sound of it.

"That still doesn't answer the question of why Rodriguez was so secretive."

*　　*　　*

Thomas had trouble sleeping. Concern over what they would find was at the forefront of his thoughts. But Taffa-Lee's questions wouldn't go away. It didn't make any sense to conceal the situation. The more people knew about it, the quicker the answers could be found.

He got up and made his way to the living/eating area. The night would be long. With the lighting in the area at one quarter, the room looked eerie. He noticed Martha-Key was sitting with some tea. His curiosity pulled him to a chair across from her.

"Are you on watch?" He asked.

"Yes."

"What are you working on?"

"I'm making notes on what I need to do tomorrow."

"Like what?"

She turned her cold stare at him. "A multi-channel com-loop link dual mode reciprocity test of the frogging repeaters."

"Sounds good."

"You don't know what that means, do you?" She smirked.

"No, I don't. I do know what a frogging repeater is."

"Really?"

"Yeah. A frogging repeater is a communication link that leaps over the barrier between normal space and Q-space. And that's how we can communicate."

"Very good." Her expression softened. "Most systems have at least two sets of repeaters orbiting the star, or stars, on two axes. Somewhere around the third or fourth planetary orbit. This increases the chance that at least one will be always in a line-of-sight position. Do you know why we need frogging repeaters?"

"No, not really."

"Because a quantum entanglement doesn't work in Q-space. That's one of the reasons why they call it quirky space. Not everything works the same as in normal space. As you know, quantum entanglement is the heart of our communications. A ship approaching a planet needs to make contact, so we use old fashion RF energy through a frogging repeater."

"Yea, that's what I thought." But Thomas couldn't hold it in and burst out laughing and Martha-Key joined in. It felt good to let go, and Martha-Key seemed to enjoy his attempt at humor.

"So, what is this test you're going to do?"

"You can initiate a self-test of all four repeaters, the two here and the two in Q-space, by transmitting one of the transponder codes, and the test sequence number. The signal traverses the barrier through all channels in a loop."

"I thought that the frogging repeaters were stable and reliable. Do you suspect something?"

"No, this gives us a simple way of comparing the results against its internal diagnostic log. It's a routine test that could put our minds to rest about tampering."

"Did you choose to stay?" Thomas hoped to catch Martha-Key off guard, to see if her expression gave any hint of her feelings.

"No," she said without flinching.

"Then who did?"

"Didn't Taffa-Lee explain? About Lee-Hope I mean."

"No. What about her?"

"She's the reason we're still here."

"How could that be? She's a little girl. Do you put that much weight on her advice?"

"Well, after all, it's her ship."

"What do you mean?" Thomas wasn't sure how to react.

"Would you like a fresh cup of tea?" She got up.

"No thank you. I'm still hoping to get some sleep."

Martha-Key returned with her cup.

"I give up. How did Lee-Hope come to own the ship?" Thomas asked.

"Lee-Hope's grandparents, actually Ned's parents, entered into a business arrangement. Another couple, who put up most of the money would be silent partners. Ned's family would run the business."

"Well then it belongs to Ned and Taffa-Lee, not Lee-Hope."

"Not really. It's not paid off yet. The contract states ownership will go to the married descendants of the two families when the loan is paid off. That will be when Lee-Hope is about forty-five or so."

"That long? That's three generations to buy a ship."

"These ships are very expensive." Martha-Key stirred her cup, steam rising from the contents. "It's not so much the size. This one's small. But this equipment easily triples the cost. You'll find most human vessels are owned by large partnerships. Few are privately owned."

"So, at that time Lee-Hope and the other couple take ownership."

"What, other couple? It's been arranged for Lee-Hope to marry the descendant of the other family." She took a long drink.

Thomas had heard of such elaborate deals. In a universe where long-term investment could mean the survival of a species, humans had adapted.

"Does Lee-Hope know about this? Is she willing to accept this stranger as her husband?"

"Yeah. He's really a nice kid. They'll make a cute couple."

"Just because Lee-Hope will someday own the ship, she can tell Ned and Taffa-Lee what to do?" It didn't seem right to Thomas.

"Not exactly. She convinced us to stay. You see, Thomas, we were all very close to that decision. She pushed us over the edge."

Thomas said, a goodnight, and went back to bed. He had new things to think about. Images of Lee-Hope all grown up and performing the day-to-day activities, as he had observed her mother doing haunted him. He finally resolved that she would do very well in her predestined future.

*　*　*

A small bright light fell on the crate in front of Victor. The rest of the tiny room was drenched in murky shadow. He gently placed the book in the center of the deep red cloth. Carefully, he wrapped the material into a neat package. He took his time making each fold precise and deliberate. A black binding then secured the entire bundle.

Victor had thought long and hard about what he had started. The moment felt right, but how could, he be sure? The old saying seemed to apply.

Only after starting a rockslide do you find out the true dangers.

He had tossed the first stone and turning back wasn't an option.

Kneeling on the floor, he cradled the package next to his chest. It had taken him his entire life to obtain what he possessed, at that moment, and he had all he needed. Hoping he was right seemed so inadequate.

"I'm ready," he said, so he could hear it, as well as the two figures engulfed in darkness by the door.

He walked out of the room for the last time and the dark figures followed.

CHAPTER 7

"Namaste, Mr. McCormick," Lee-Hope said, as she pounded on his door. "Breakfast is ready."

Thomas didn't care. The food during this watch hadn't set well, too much like the chili he had the first day. He preferred the middle and late meals. He decided some tea would help and got up anyway. The restless night made him feel more tired than when he had gone to sleep. However, the others appeared rested and ready. After the meal, Rusty had placed a fresh pot of tea on the table and Ned posed a question.

"What could be done to this pot so that I couldn't see it?" His eyes stared at the shiny metal utilitarian ball with a lid and spout until distracted by a small hand.

"I know," Lee-Hope waved.

"Yes, go on." Ned looked pleased.

Lee-Hope unfolded a napkin she used at breakfast. She placed it over the object, then sat down, confident in her action.

"Very good. It's hidden." Ned reached out and put his fingers next to the cloth. "But I detect something warm behind this." He smiled at Lee-Hope.

This had all been done for her benefit. Thomas realized what good people they were to involve their child, not only to include her as part of the family business, but in the process of problem-solving and planning the work.

"If the planet hasn't moved then it's hidden. I feel this is the most likely possibility." Ned quickly looked around the table. "That's our best chance of finding it."

"Why do you count out the other two alternatives?" Rusty asked.

"If Bohica had moved a little, we would have seen it. If it had moved a lot, we would have a much bigger area to search. The chances of finding it are smaller."

"What if it were blown up or vaporized?" Thomas asked.

"That's the third possibility. But we'd see debris everywhere, and even if it was vaporized our instruments would go crazy. It would be hard to ignore such a cataclysmic event."

"One problem with your theory," Rusty said, "is that as far as I know no one has found a way to cover gravimetric reading from these detectors. You can't hide gravity."

"Well maybe something has. If so, let's hope it's a new widget that's imperfect."

"As Ned explained, it seems the best place to start," Taffa-Lee added.

"Let's also hope that it's not a combination of these ideas. You know, moved then hidden." Rusty wasn't convinced it would be that easy to find.

"Let's hope not. I want to remind everyone to attach all methods, procedures, protocols and raw data to the findings of each series we run before we give it to Thomas. I don't want anybody saying the *Gold Rat* has sloppy records. Let's get to work."

Everyone else got up and went about their tasks. Thomas stayed seated feeling better and more optimistic than he had for days. Finally, Angelica-So's fate would be resolved. They would find out what happened. He could then face Charm even with bad news as the outcome. He was no longer the alien and was again on a first-name basis with the crew.

Ned came back and sat next to him. "You know, Thomas, there is something you could do."

"Good. I've felt useless so far. But I don't understand all this technical stuff. You'll have to make it easy on me."

"Can't do that. It's not technical, but it will take work." Ned's face showed signs of concern as he nervously played with a teacup. "I've been worried about who would do this and why."

"It's been in my thoughts also." Thomas knew where this was going.

"I would like you to use whatever influence you have to poke around and get some answers."

"All right, I can do that."

After Ned returned to his work, Thomas thought about whom to talk to and what to ask them. He knew he needed to report to Rodriguez but wanted to put it off a while longer.

Thomas went to see Martha-Key. "Did you run that test on the repeaters you were working on last night?"

"Yes." She brought up a new screen on her terminal to show him. "The reciprocity delay is a bit high, but everything is within spec."

"Good, I'm going to do some communication. Can you make sure I have a channel to my terminal?"

"You're patched in," she said. But before he could turn away, she spoke. "Thomas." It was almost a whisper.

"What?" He asked, leaning forward.

"You remember our conversation about Lee-Hope last night?"

"Yes."

"I probably shouldn't have said anything about it."

"Why did you?"

"I don't know."

"No problem. Let me know if anyone finds something," Thomas said, then he went back to his cabin.

He went through lists of names of old contacts, associates, ex employers and just people he'd meet over his lifetime. Most were humans with limited influence, but many were aliens. Thomas knew a larger variety of creatures than most people. It pleased him to know he got along and could deal with them fairly and honestly. Most humans just hated them and didn't want any kind of contact. Thomas never understood that. They were here and couldn't be ignored. It even made sense to start his search there.

He also gave thought to the questions to ask that would get answers and not alarm anyone about the problem. The words of Taffa-Lee still haunted him. Could the director be holding something back? And yet, he couldn't shake the directive from Rodriguez. To say nothing.

At the end of the second watch, when Lee-Hope announced the meal, Thomas only knew frustration. If anybody knew anything about

Bohica they were unwilling to discuss it. Most of them just didn't know what he was talking about.

Sitting at the table in Operations, Thomas wanted to know what they had found.

"Please, Thomas, let's eat first," Taffa-Lee said.

"I'm very anxious to see what you found."

"We need this time to relax," she replied.

"Look, I just want to know . . ." Thomas looked down, a small hand rested on his arm.

"We'll eat first," Lee-hope said.

The general tension seemed to be running higher than normal. What could have happened or not happened to put these people so on edge? This only heightened Thomas' curiosity. Lee-Hope slid a bowl into his hands and gave him a soft smile. He decided to exercise his often-unused patience.

Everyone did seem more pleasant after the vegetable stew and rice.

"It didn't look good today, Thomas," Taffa-Lee stated.

"I take it you didn't find it."

"We had no indications at all. Everything we tried was a wash," Rusty added.

"Tomorrow we'll take some other measurements. Rusty came up with one I think will be very revealing. The *Monkey Fist* will move to the side of the planet, with respect to us. They will then fire their energy weapon at where we think Bohica should be."

"Wait a minute, what if you hit the colony?"

"The planet is just a big rock," Rusty said, "and 99 percent of the habitation is underground. Not to worry, the *Monkey Fist* will fire at maximum dispersion. The effect will be just a little ionization of the dust on the surface. But we'll pick up the back scatter radiation, surface disturbance, and a score of other things with our detectors. The data will read like a cookbook."

"We'll serve Bohica for breakfast," Taffa-Lee said, smiling.

At the start of the following watch Thomas couldn't pull himself away from watching what he had come to think of as the cookbook test. He stood by and watched as the *Gold Rat's* crew did seemingly endless adjustments and checks. During his fourth cup of tea, he began to understand how tightly they worked together.

Lee-Hope sat at a terminal at the far end of the equipment. She motioned Thomas to join her.

"We can watch everything from here. I'll show you."

She pointed to a display of a real-time picture of empty space with a simple graphic globe.

"Is that where Bohica should be?" Asked Thomas.

"That's right." She moved her finger to a small dot on the left side. "And that is the *Monkey's Fist*."

"They're in position," Ned reported.

"Kert, are you charged up and ready to go?" Taffa-Lee asked, a young man's picture appeared on a display.

"We're set and waiting for your signal," he replied.

"Are all detectors and recorders on?"

"Yes," Rusty replied.

Thomas couldn't remember staring any harder at anything before in his life. His eyes strained.

"You may fire Kert."

A small false-color red pattern appeared in the center of where the planet should have been. It grew in intensity, then faded. Unimpressed with the sight, Thomas turned to Rusty.

"Is that what you expected?"

"No," Taffa-Lee whispered, staring at the image on her terminal.

"What does this mean?"

"It was just a tiny dust cloud." Rusty looked numb. "Bohica isn't here. It's gone."

"I already knew that." Thomas couldn't believe all this work and effort to discover what he already knew. He went back to his cabin, more depressed than ever.

*   *   *

The crew of the *Gold Rat* had little to add in the next two days. Thomas spent most of his time alone. His contact with the rest of the crew aboard the ship became minimal, and he sensed an ever-increasing tension. The one exception was Lee-Hope's earnest attempt to make his stay comfortable.

"Mr. McCormick, we need you in operations."

"Okay, give me five minutes."

He walked in on the end of the third day's meeting period to discuss the findings of that shift and talk over the plans for the next day. He had missed the last two.

"Well, I think that's the only thing left," Ned said to Rusty with the most optimism Thomas had seen since they arrived. Ned gestured to Rusty to continue.

"Thomas, I think we have a way to solve this puzzle."

"I'm anxious to hear about it."

"What we intend to do is go back in time to before the disappearance of Bohica. Then we can watch it all happen in real time. After that we should know what happened and what to do."

"Are you crazy?" Thomas couldn't believe what he was hearing. "The last information I recall before coming on this trip was that nobody could go back in time. That's still a pipe dream. Maybe you could do some minor localized temporal shifts in the laboratory under controlled conditions. But going back a few standard weeks is madness."

"Please Thomas, calm down," Taffa-Lee said. She looked genuinely concerned.

"How do you expect to get back in time? Have you got H. G. Wells as a Stowaway somewhere?"

Rusty put a smile on his sheepish face. "Take it easy, Thomas, the only problem we have is that we can't get to there from here."

*   *   *

Victor sat cross-legged on his bunk, as the familiar hum of the ship's systems droned in the background. Sitting on the soft mattress, he felt the vibration of the engines as they strained to push the vessel forward.

The red cloth spread out over his lap. The book's old yellow pages yearned for his understanding. Being more comfortable than usual, along with the noise, annoyed him. He had to work at concentrating. He found the passage he sought.

Li Ch'uan: 'Weapons are tools of ill omen.' War is a grave matter; one is apprehensive lest men embark upon it without due reflection.

Victor next reviewed the five fundamental factors. Despite logic, reason and history, he refused to change his mind. The machinery he had set in motion would stay upon the path. Mercy to the ones that will not move.

He reached over to the terminal next to his bed and keyed it for communication. A familiar face appeared. It was old with wrinkles, but with kind and searching eyes.

"Victor, what has taken you so long? We are all standing around holding our breath."

"You must learn to relax. The first step is to breathe." Victor used just enough sarcasm to goad his old friend.

"Very funny. We have reconsidered your information and feel the timing is wrong."

"No. Have you thought about it? You're not going to like it if I'm right." Victor was afraid they might change their minds. Too many years huddled in the dark and your knees get weak.

"We've thought about it and we're sticking with our first reaction."

"Are you sure? If you're wrong, it will be a mess for everyone. It'll be even worse if we don't act now." His voice rose with annoyance. "It is time to beat the drum and light the fires. You must trust me, my old friend."

The face in the terminal smiled back at him. "Sorry, Victor, the timing is wrong."

"I'm on my way. Maybe I can convince you in person."

"You're welcome here any time. You know that. But I don't think it will do much good."

After the terminal went dark, Victor rubbed his eyes and hoped he had made the right decision. Had he been too hasty? Too many variables were unclear. His thoughts were drawn back to the book. The passages continued to haunt him.

ENERGY 14: When the strike of a hawk breaks the body of its prey, it is because of timing.

CHAPTER 8

"Namaste," the Director said, with a touch of distaste. "Where the hell have you been?"

Thomas had taken the opportunity of the *Gold Rat's* short return to Q-space to contact Rodriguez.

"I don't have a lot of time. I'm going to send you every file we have on the situation. It looks bad. In fact, . . .," Thomas felt ashamed to speak in absurdities, "the planet Bohica is not even here."

"What are you talking about?"

Thomas did his best to convince Rodriguez of what he knew. Though difficult for anyone to believe, Rodriguez finally accepted Thomas' story.

"It wasn't supposed to happen like this."

"What do you mean?" Thomas asked, sensing more behind the statement.

"You know, having our plan turn out right instead of getting kicked around, like normal." The Director's gaze drifted off. He made eye contact one more time. "Thank you, Thomas," he said, then terminated the transmission.

Perfect timing. The ship resounded with a thump on the hull, announcing that the *Gold Rat* had popped into normal space. It didn't take very long to travel a standard light week in Q-space, or should he say travel back in time a week. He had been so gullible. He believed what Ned and Rusty said, going back in time at the same point in space.

"Mr. McCormick?" A small voice called on the other side of his cabin door. "Rusty is deploying the optical scope. We have ten minutes."

"I'll be right there."

It involved a simple process. Go to a spot where the light of the incident at Bohica hasn't reached yet. Then sit down and watch the event as it unfolds in real time. For most people, it's like looking at the stars in the night sky. What they see are the stars of many years ago. Light takes that long to travel that far. But it's not so common for humans. Ninety-five percent of humanity lives underground. Some may glimpse the stars only a few times during their life.

The only way you can do this, of course, is to travel in Q-space. That quirky little place that is much smaller than our universe and yet at the same time touches every point of our universe. So, instead of taking a year at the speed of light to reach a star, you pop into Q-Space for a couple of days at one G to reach that same star.

Everyone huddled around the displays and took their first look at Bohica. The gray lump of rock that had eluded them showed large on the screen. They all felt relieved that the question of their sanity had been resolved. Thomas, however, found his breathing had quickened.

"Right there," Rusty said, with an edge of surprise, as he zoomed in the display, "two ships. That one is the colonies' shuttle and the other is the freighter, *Clipper VI* - contracted to resupply the colony."

"It all looks normal enough," Ned commented.

"And there," Rusty pointed to a spot on the planet with his little finger, "that is the colony itself."

Thomas could barely control his excitement. He wanted to do something to stop whatever was coming. To warn Angelica-So and the others of the danger, but he couldn't. His hands shook. It had already happened. There was nothing to do but watch and let the sadness overcome him.

"Look," Taffa-Lee screamed. "Ships just popped into the system."

Everyone's attention shifted to a display showing a wider view. The planet could be covered with your thumb. They saw the markers of three ships moving toward Bohica. Taffa-Lee quickly changed the display on one of the smaller monitors.

"They're all at three-hundred-thousand kilometers from the surface."

"The report said that there were four ships," Thomas said.

"The fourth one must be on the far side, hidden from the sensors by Bohica."

"Two-hundred-thousand kilometers."

"Am I crazy, or are they accelerating toward the planet?"

"Yes."

"What?"

"You're not. And yes, they are. One-hundred-thousand kilometers."

Thomas couldn't help but wonder about Angelica. For Thomas, she had become the image of everyone at the colony. What was she doing? Was she happy or frightened? And the haunting question that refused to be satisfied, was she still alive?

"Fifty-thousand kilometers. Are we picking up any information from them?" Taffa-Lee asked.

"None," Rusty replied. "But they are using gravity and thrusters to accelerate."

"Five-thousand kilometers."

"Any moment now they'll impact on the surface."

But they never reached the planet. In an instant, everything disappeared. It was gone. A blank screen. Taffa-Lee gasped, and Rusty quickly checked his settings in a panic.

"No, this can't be. It doesn't make any sense!" Rusty yelled as he sprang up and began to pace. "It's too quick. You can't do it that fast. It's a trick."

"Please calm down. You're scaring me." Martha-Key gently took Rusty's arm. "We'll find out what it is. You've got to get a hold of yourself."

Thomas turned away from the monitors and found Lee-Hope standing behind him.

"Where there's no sense there's no feeling," she whispered, her eyes staring into the distance of the blank screen.

"You've recorded this, right?" Thomas asked. "Can't you play it back slower so we can see if there's more information?"

"Yes, Thomas, we'll do that," Taffa-Lee said, "but it will take a while to analyze the data. Is that okay with you?"

"Of course," Thomas replied, as nicely as he could with his whole body shaking.

Later, Thomas found himself sitting with a calmer but more irritated Rusty. They were viewing the optical image recorded earlier. He understood what Rusty was going through. Thomas had been there three days ago. He had moved onto frustration and a dulling of his senses.

"Here we are." Rusty manipulated the terminal. An image of Bohica filled the screen. "We sample and store all detector readings at intervals. The faster we sample, the better we know what's going on. We were sampling this image at one thousand times a standard second. That's about as fast as we can record a complete set of detector outputs for any length of time." Rusty pointed to the screen.

"This is a magnified sample before the incident." Bohica's gray mass appeared as they had seen it before. Rusty adjusted the terminal. "This is the next sample."

Thomas stared at a screen filled with background stars.

"Whatever happened took less than one millisecond. We could go back out there and try it again at a faster rate with a single type of detector. But if I don't know what to look for and the time frame, we could be out here for months."

"Does this give us any better understanding of what might have happened here?"

"No." Rusty said, looking tired. "We just have more questions."

"Thomas?" Ned intruded into the conversation. "The *Assegai* has just told us that another ship has entered the Bohica system. They're requesting that we return and meet with them."

"Tell me, Ned," Thomas said, standing up to face him. "Does any of this information get us closer to an answer?"

"No."

"Maybe we should leave then."

On the way back to the system the *Assegai* learned that the other ship was the *Cape York*, a passenger liner with refugees from Tuska.

"The Captain of the *Cape York* knows that we're on our way and that you will arrive shortly. That is, you being a Union Rep, he is demanding to meet with you." Ned seemed almost apologetic.

"Of course, I understand," said Thomas.

"I plan to dock with the liner as soon as we enter the system, if that's all right with you."

"That will be fine, Ned." Thomas had no idea what he would say or if he could do anything to help. He found himself in situations he hadn't prepared for or expected.

*   *   *

"Thank you, Captain," the Group Master said. The Captain left and the Green lizard entered the busy communication room and waited to approach him. "Have the *Rock-Ten* link up with us and brief them. That will be all."

"Admiral, have we news from the mammals?" The green marble skinned lizard asked with an air of apprehension.

"No. And that is the problem. They have been fumbling around out there far too long. They should have made some simple connections to what has happened by now." The Group Master slowly walked around the perimeter of the room, looking at the displays and information consoles.

"That's unfortunate. I had hoped it wouldn't take long." The Green lizard followed a half-step behind.

The noise of the machinery and a flock of Tri-Bah talking with each other made for hectic surroundings. The Group Master hoped that the communication center would keep his guest off guard. He wanted the upper hand whenever possible and pretended to pay more attention to the flashing lights than the conversation.

"I've decided to be less cryptic about what happened," said the Group Master. "Sharing information with these animals should move the timetable along. I have a task for you."

"For me? I'm the guest of the Tri-Bah Nest. You can't order me to do your job."

"Of course, I'm not going to make you do anything. But I would expect you to be eager to find out how these mammals think and why it is taking them so long." The Group Master rubbed his jaw with the two thumbs of his left paw.

"As intriguing as that would be, it might reveal my kind too soon."

"If I were to send anyone else, it would expose much more. Your species is nebulous to everyone around here. An unknown and a mystery. You are the perfect messenger."

*   *   *

Thomas stepped through the airlock and into the *Cape York*. Everything seemed a little bigger and roomier. A ship catering to passengers required more comfort. Thomas shook hands with the Captain as he entered a small dining area. He guessed it was the crew's mess.

"This is a very nice ship. You don't see many human-owned passenger liners." Thomas wanted to start the conversation on a complimentary note.

"Thank you. There are some passengers who insist on traveling in the care of humans, mostly other humans. Mr. McCormick, I have two hundred and forty-seven people to deliver to Bohica. And I find out that it's no longer here. What am I going to do with these refugees? And where's Bohica?"

"I don't know what to tell you."

"Well, the Union is organizing this venture, and you're the Representative. So let us know where to take them."

"I'll get in touch with Administration on Ichorous, and find out what we can do," Thomas said, realizing he didn't need another job.

"I blame the Union for relinquishing the colony on Tuska before the contract expired. They should never have done that. This is the third time in sixty years we've been kicked off a planet before the time was up." The Captain seemed truly upset.

"I'm sorry, but I have had nothing to do with Tuska." Thomas began to feel defensive. The Captain was right, of course, but Thomas didn't like it.

"Yes, Mr. McCormick. But the workers have done a great job. Material has been delivered on schedule. The humans have contributed to the infrastructure expansion of that planet far beyond what the contract required. It's just not fair, to displace twelve-thousand people on a whim."

"I'm sure they had a reason." Thomas could only think of one and he was sure it was the same as what the Captain thought.

"Yes, to stop us from expanding up the spiral arm. Do you know whom they're bringing in to replace us?"

"I was under the impression the work was completed."

"No, far from it. They're having Keets finish the job. Can you believe that? Keets are not reliable workers." The Captains' voice got lower.

"We seem to be getting off the subject here." Thomas couldn't argue with the man or his facts.

"Let me tell you about the subject. I'm carrying deep miners and their families. They're here to expand the living quarters on Bohica for the other three shiploads behind me. The idea is to double the colony in the next few weeks."

Thomas didn't have a response.

"And where in hell is Bohica anyway?" the Captain's voice had crept even louder.

Ned stood in the doorway, "Excuse me, Thomas, Rodriguez needs to talk with you, right away."

CHAPTER 9

"Namaste, Director," Thomas said. "I didn't expect to hear from you so soon."

"You need to go to Fallen."

"Why, has that planet disappeared also?" Thomas regretted saying that as soon as it came out of his mouth.

"I'm serious, Thomas." Rodriguez's face didn't change with the attempt at humor. "Our liaison will meet you there. He'll escort you to the proper location."

"Has he been briefed?"

"Yes."

"And why am I going there?"

"To meet with someone who has information about Bohica. I'm sending you the details," said Rodriguez.

"While I have you, the *Cape York* has just arrived from Tuska. What are we going to do about these people?"

"Don't worry about that. You just get to Fallen." The Director's image disappeared.

"That's easy for you to say." But the blank screen didn't answer. He couldn't believe he had yet another place to run off to. What would he tell the Captain of the *Cape York*? Thomas went looking for Ned.

"Why don't you take the *Monkey's Fist*? It's a little faster. We'll stay here and continue the search. We have a mass distribution measurement we'd like to do."

"Haven't you done that?"

"This test is more accurate and covers a much larger area. It involves deploying eight remote detectors, calibrations of the array and taking a series of measurements. After that we retrieve the remote detectors. The whole procedure takes a couple of days. With you gone we can take the time to do it and should be done when you get back."

"What's so different about this test?"

"We'll have the mass reading on a quarter of a cubic parsec. If Bohica has been moved anywhere near that space it will show up on our sensors."

"It sounds like a good opportunity to do that."

"One more thing." Ned looked apprehensive, almost apologetic.

"What is it?"

"Three more ships have entered the system."

"Who are they? Is there a danger?" Thomas felt his body tense.

"No, not at all. Two came in a while ago and one just arrived. I think they are curious," Ned said.

"I want to talk to them," said Thomas.

Martha-Key set up the communication while Thomas put on his best business face in front of a terminal. First were a couple of Keet yachts that were passing by. Their crews wanted to know if all the rumors were true. They were leaving shortly.

The other was a human-owned container vessel. Also hearing rumors of a disaster, they did what any good ship would and stopped to help.

"I assure you, Captain Orzo, there is no need for you to stay. The Union appreciates and commends your willingness to help. It reflects well on you to show such dedication to helping other humans in need. However, I can report that everything is well in hand and there is no need for your involvement."

"You're welcome, Mr. McCormick. We will pass this way in a week. We'll check in with you, just to make sure."

"That will be fine. You and your crew have a safe trip."

"Thank you. And good luck to you, Sir." Thomas felt sick. Never had diplomacy sounded so two-faced.

*　*　*

The *Tank Man* popped into the most hectic system Victor had ever known. Three separate asteroid belts circled the dim binary stars. The planets that were left didn't stay in a nice flat orbital plain. They were as chaotic and distorted as any place he had ever seen. A hundred times the comet activity of an average system made it a mess. But it was home.

He had no time to visit. Docking with an ordinary looking rock in the third belt, Victor soon found himself on his way through small narrow hallways to meet the man that had brought him there. He braced himself for an argument. He had to make them rethink their position.

"Victor, you old weasel, it's good to see you. It has been too long. Come in and sit down." Victors' friend indicated a comfortable looking chair.

"You must reconsider." Pleasantries were the farthest thing from Victors' mind. His old friend had to understand the importance of the situation.

"But we have."

"What?"

"We received some disturbing rumors and diverted a courier ship to verify the report."

Victor sensed the change in his friend. "What did you find?"

"It's what we didn't find that has us worried."

*   *   *

Lee-Hope insisted on carrying his bag to the airlock. She took her job very seriously.

"I hope you have enjoyed your stay on the *Gold Rat* and will join us again soon," she said, with uncommon professionalism.

"I'm only going for a day or two. I'll be right back."

"I know." She smiled. "I'm supposed to say that."

"And you did it very well," Thomas said as he took his bag.

Thomas stepped through the airlock and shook hands with the two occupants of the smaller ship.

"Hello, Mr. McCormick, I'm Kert and this is my brother Keil."

"Call me Thomas."

"Welcome. We're a little cramped, but please relax and have a seat."

The insides of the *Monkey's Fist* had a deceptively spacious feel. Besides a storage bay and a lavatory, the living compartment took up most of the room. Propulsion, weapon systems and life support made up the rest of the ship.

Kert and Keil were identical twins with short cropped blond hair and a lanky look. The two got to work and made the jump quickly. After a time of monitoring the progress, one turned from the console.

"We just have to wait until we get there."

The brothers started talking together quietly at first but got louder as time went on. The discussion turned into an ongoing argument.

"Well, I'm sorry, I think we need more than one," said Keil.

"You're asking for trouble," replied Kert.

"No, if we did it your way, it would be more trouble."

"How can you say that?"

The brothers realized the argument had disturbed Thomas.

"Excuse our manners but we're not used to having people around. We just blurt out what's on our minds."

"I understand. This is your ship. You should do whatever is normal." Thomas tried to make himself comfortable on one of the bunks he had been offered.

"Thank you," they both said.

"Why don't we ask our guest?"

"Good idea."

"We understand that you have settled many arguments and done some arbitration."

Thomas didn't know if he wanted to get involved with a family dispute. But as a captive audience he didn't have much choice.

"Yes, I have."

"Would you listen to our disagreement and advise us on what you think is best?"

"I won't promise good advice, but I'll hear you out. If it's not too controversial, I'll offer you my opinion," Thomas said, pleased that he had left himself a way out if it got sticky.

"You see Thomas. It's like this. We belong to a Surrien consortium that provides transportation security. Its family owned and very profitable. We're at a point where we have an opportunity to move to a bigger ship."

"What my brother is trying to say is that we are ready to get married and need to move into a roomier vessel to start families."

"Yeah, that's it," the other said.

"Sounds good, I'm married and can recommend it. What's the problem?" Thomas asked.

"Well, Keil thinks we should get two wives, one for each of us. I, on the other hand, think we only need one. It will be far less conducive to jealousy."

"No, it won't," Kert insisted. "If we each had our own, there would be less to be jealous about. We wouldn't be fighting over the same thing,"

"You would prefer us to fight over two different things. That gives us twice as much to fight over."

"Not that again."

"Thomas, doesn't it make sense? If you had two wives, one will be prettier that the other, one nicer, one smarter, one more enjoyable to be with and one that cooks better. All these differences have the potential of causing jealousy."

Thomas wasn't sure what to say. He had to spend the next couple of days with these two and didn't want to have them both mad at him.

"Admit it. If we had two wives one would be better than the other," said Kert

"Excuse me, Kert, but if we had only one then I would be jealous when she is with you, and you would be jealous when she's with me."

The twins' hands became more animated.

"It doesn't have to be that way."

"But it will."

"No, it won't."

"Yes."

"Wait a minute." Thomas had to stop this for his own sanity's sake.

"We're sorry."

"What do you think, one wife or two?"

"Draw match sticks, roll the dice or pick a number. It doesn't matter," Thomas said politely.

The brothers looked at each other and then at Thomas, "What's a matchstick?"

"Whatever you decide will work or fail, depending on the time and effort you put into it."

"But what should we do?"

"Just get married. By the time you have kids, you'll be in so much trouble that this argument will be forgotten."

Thomas stretched out on the bunk to get some rest. He had to give them some credit. Most people would run off and do the first thing that came into their head without investigating the consequences of their actions. At least they were talking and that was good as long as it wasn't at him.

He realized their schedule would put him planet-side at the wrong time, right in the middle of his sleep routine. Just what he needed, to be at a critical meeting with hyper-lag.

He also couldn't seem to relax. The events of the last few days kept turning over in his mind. So many pieces, and none of them fit. Three things reemerged over and over. The vision of Bohica disappearing on the terminal in front of him. The words of Rodriguez, *It's not supposed to happen this way.* And the whispers of Lee-Hope, *"Where there's no sense, there's no feeling."*

Kert and Keil were quieter during the remainder of the trip to Fallen.

Thomas wondered what new wrinkles he could look forward to.

CHAPTER 10

"Namaste, did you rest well?"

"Yes," Victor lied, not wanting to offend his good friend's hospitality. He had time to get a few hours of sleep, but he felt restless not rested. The revelations he learned were disturbing and the stuff to nurture childish nightmares.

"Good. Everyone has agreed that you should contact this representative . . ." His friend looked at a terminal on his Spartan desk, "Thomas McCormick. We need to know exactly what's going on before we commit 100 percent."

"I disagree. You should be able to trust me by now." Victor's old thick skin felt the sting of the barb. Normally he wouldn't care. But he could feel being right.

"Listen, Victor, it's not a matter of trust. You should know that. We believe that you are sincere. It's just that we should move only if the situation calls for it and not on a whim."

Victor was tired of this argument. It wasn't the one he came for. "So, you want me to go and be your spy again."

"That's what you do best." His friend gave him a big grin.

"You had better be ready."

"We will. Preparations have been under way since before you arrived. We're treating this like a drill. Only this time everybody is involved. We will be in lurking mode by the time you know anything for sure. And I bet you a fiver that it will all be for nothing."

Victor stood up, giving his friend a smile. He extended his hand. "We'll see."

*   *   *

"Thomas. Wake up. We're landing."

The *Monkey's Fist* didn't require a shuttle. It could land directly onto most planets. By the time they were down, Thomas had pulled himself together and looked presentable. Of course, he didn't feel it, that would take a lot longer. He hadn't slept well. Nightmare visions of Charm and Angelica haunted him. Terrible things happened to them, and he was helpless to prevent it. Being awake made the dreams go away but not the reality. Which one was the worse?

He'd hoped today would be better. That depended on what he learned. To make this trip productive he needed some major new information.

"We were told as we approached that your contact is waiting in staging area seven. He also said that if you hurry, you'll be on time for the meeting," said Keil.

"We'll be waiting here whenever you're done. Do you think we'll have time after your meeting? We could use a few hours for some maintenance and refitting."

"I'm not sure. I don't see why not, unless something extraordinary happens."

Thomas walked down the ramp leading from the air lock of the *Monkey's Fist* and made his way to the staging area. The port at Fallen roared with the activity of commerce. The atmosphere of Fallen had little oxygen. So, the port was inside a mountain. Cargo was moving about, maintenance crews were working on a variety of ships, and every kind of creature was going somewhere. For a moment Thomas regretted not growing a beard, but his decision only made him proud to be human.

"Representative McCormick?"

"Yes." Thomas turned to find a young human running up to him.

He was dressed in business attire, with a small decorative knife at his side, and had a well-trimmed goatee. It was the fashion of the younger humans. He reminded Thomas of his son.

"Welcome to Fallen. My name is George of the Union of Humanity Contingent. I have transportation over here."

They got onto a small open vehicle that George moved freely through the confusion of the staging floor. He managed to miss almost everything. After turning down a long corridor, it settled into a smooth ride.

"So, Mr. McCormick, is it true?"

"Is what true?"

"You know. Did something terrible happen? All we have gotten are rumors about Bohica. And those have been vague."

"Don't you know? Being an official in a highly commercial trading center so close to Bohica, I'd think they would have told you." This disturbed Thomas.

"No. They don't tell me anything."

"I was under the impression you were briefed."

"Sorry."

Thomas didn't like any of this. Did he misunderstand Rodriguez? Or could he trust this guy with the smart goatee? He had become suspicious of everyone. This paranoia could color his judgment. He must remain objective and hope he doesn't see red.

"What did you hear?" Thomas decided to ask.

"Some say that Bohica has been attacked by the Tri-Bah or marauders. Others say there's been a natural disaster." He leaned a little closer and lowered his voice. "I've even heard that Bohica has disappeared completely," he laughed.

Thomas also laughed. He couldn't help himself. Stated out loud, it sounded so ridiculous.

George stopped in front of an opening carved into the stone. The rough surface became smoother as it got closer to the arched doorway. Words in blue light appeared on either side of the entrance. The name of the establishment seemed only to be 'WELCOME' in twenty different languages, only a few of them Thomas recognized.

"Whom am I meeting here?"

"I have no idea. But they will contact you. I'll wait here. And good luck, sir."

Thomas got out of the vehicle but hesitated at the entrance. He thought again about what had brought him there and reconfirmed his determination to find out the truth about Angelica's fate. *It's time to move forward*, he thought, walking into the noisy room.

No matter how many thousands of light years away from home Thomas traveled, all the space port bars look the same. The place was filled with snorting, growling, and hissing, make-you-sick-to-your-stomach aliens. Only this place had a unique smell of the aroma of an old duffel bag.

There were few humans among the colder blooded patrons. To his relief, there were no insectoids. Even Thomas couldn't stand bugs. Despite his revulsion for this kind of place, it wasn't that bad. It wasn't like there were many human-only bars this high up the spiral arm. He realized he could use a drink. No, he needed a drink. Thomas felt like he had been rattling around in a tin can. Not that the *Monkey's Fist* and *Gold Rat* weren't decently good ships. It felt good to stretch his legs.

This was a 'Free' bar. Not what most inexperienced travelers thought, the drinks and food were not free. No. This bar was free to establish its own rules. This could be anything from complete anarchy to absolute dictatorship. Many of these types of places were limited to regulating weapons.

Most of the time the establishment confiscated all weapons. There was one place he had been during a business trip, where weapons were taken from only the species that had such things as claws and teeth that could rip someone apart. Everyone else was allowed to keep their knifes, guns, hugracs, or whatever else they had.

Thomas checked in his Kanashimi knife and informed the hairy mammal running the establishment what he wanted. He looked for a place to sit. Scattered around the bar was a variety of furniture, apparatuses and some structures designed for creatures to relax upon. One small table half surrounded by a couch-like form seemed inviting. He took care making his way through the room. He didn't want to step on any tails, trip over appendages or do anything that would lead to misunderstandings. You know, common bar room etiquette.

Before sitting Thomas carefully inspected the cushions for parasites or slime left by some careless creature. The seat was comfortable, but he preferred a lower ion count and higher humidity. A good drink could make up for this kind of discomfort. His last drink had been at the party on Mitzul. It seemed so long ago.

Gazing around the room waiting for his drink, he remembered *The White Catalog of Sentient Species*. It had become a favorite of his as a child, back when his parents could barely afford air. Armondo and he had hours of fun painting mustaches on the animals.

A question begged to be asked in his mind as he sat amid a collection of beings lifted from that catalog. Could any of them disappear a planet? Dr. Whitman's theory of intra species intelligence might hold a clue. His theory suggested that a measurement of collective intelligence is the range between how small, and how large a conscious manipulation of his environment a species can make. For example, it's one thing to stack atoms, and change the ecology of a world. It's more difficult to construct atoms and rearrange solar systems.

Is that what had happened at Bohica? Had it been moved? Rusty thought so. For him and the crew of the *Gold Rat*, searching for what happened, there had been no clear results. It wasn't like they had lost, forgotten or misplaced it. They knew exactly where to look. It just wasn't there. They had scoured the system and found nothing to account for a planet.

Rodriguez told him to come here. This bar might have new information. Thomas didn't know why the Director of the Union would personally arrange this kind of meeting. He could take it two ways. Rodriguez might be truly concerned and wanted to resolve the situation. On the other hand, he could be hiding something. In that case it would make sense to keep the number of people involved to a minimum.

He didn't mind the task. But if the Director had something to hide, the job could have unknown dangers. Thomas wished he knew more of what to expect.

Finally, a furry-purry thing brought his Southern Fizz. He immediately realized the bartender knew nothing about mixing drinks.

Thomas's disappointment turned to anticipation as he noticed a dark green, smooth-skinned, reptile studying him from the doorway. It wore a black tunic with gold trim and carried a shallow bowl. Gracefully, it made its way toward Thomas. Many of the patrons watched it glide through the room. It stopped in front of his table. Thomas could clearly make out the gold tattoo of a snowflake just below the back of its wrist. It opened its claw with its four digits pointing down and the palm forward.

"May I join you?" He asked in a deep resonating voice.

CHAPTER 11

The Tri-Bah Group Master couldn't keep his mind on the task at hand. It should have been so easy. All officers had favorite activities of their commands. Many had their pride in the Cluster ships and the squadrons of Pebble fighters they carried. A lot had to do with how the officers came up through the ranks.

His pride centered on the assault ships and the hundreds of soldiers they carried. Inspecting these troops in the exercise hold of his number one assault ship was very important to him.

For the Tri-Bah to extend their influence throughout the systems they must, *DOMINATE THE SKY ABOVE AND THE GROUND BELOW.* It was the motto of the Tri-Bah military.

Despite doing his most loved duty, his thoughts wandered. He was glad he was alone. That green envoy was off with the human animals, and he secretly hoped it would take a long time. Could he trust that arrogant green reptile to do what he required?

He didn't like this operation. It didn't feel right. It wasn't like the leadership to act without provocation toward another species. Most of their neighbors were glad to have fire lizards around. The Tri-Bah might be the muscle in this part of space, but they didn't use it in an immoral gain for their own. After all, *Space was safe where the Group Masters reign.*

He tried to get back to a bit of normalcy. He watched a squad of soldiers run through an exercise. They moved and fired their weapons, each one as part of the team. The simulation to breach and enter another ship took on a dance-like quality. As they established and secured a safe zone, the players froze in the final moment of the performance.

The Group Master's pride in these soldiers was tainted by the taste of a word. He never thought his mighty Tri-Bah would be linked to that despicable word, immoral.

And it all centered around that arrogant green slug. It wasn't him alone, but their race. The Tri-Bah didn't need them. Why the leadership kept them around, he didn't understand.

He turned to the commander of the soldiers. "They did very well. Training keeps the weapons sharp. Give them my compliments. You're dismissed."

As the Tri-Bah authority in this part of the Spiral Arm, he made the judgments upon others and would do the tasks given him. There would be no moral dilemma.

*   *   *

Thomas pointed to the far end of the couch. He had never seen this species. The lizard stood tall, a deep green. The unmistakable snowflake design looked like gold inlaid in marble.

Placing the bowl on the table and sitting down, it looked at Thomas with large snakelike eyes. "You are human," he said.

"And you are a lizard," Thomas replied, not knowing if he asked a question, made a statement, or offered him an insult. He wanted his response to be as unrevealing.

Taking three of his four digits on his left paw, he dragged them across the bottom of the bowl. It contained a thick, yellow-green liquid that reeked of burnt rubber. The high-pitched scraping noises of claws against porcelain raised the hairs on the back of Thomas's neck.

Then, with great relish, the lizard licked the substance off his digits, using his split tongue. Watching him wrap both tips of his tongue around his claws in opposite directions at the same time was hypnotic. He repeated this process often throughout their conversation.

"Are you one of the humans looking for Bohica?" he asked, with one finger left to lick.

His polite directness removed some of Thomas' tensions. He decided to be just as straightforward. "Yes. Do you know anything about its disappearance? We could use any information that might help us understand what happened?"

"I'm curious to know what you think happened. You and your humans have been searching for quite a while. You must have some idea."

"How do you know how long we have been looking?" So, they had been watching them.

"Does it matter?"

Who are they? Thomas had never seen this kind before. And yet he's involved in dealing with humans and perhaps the Fire Lizard.

"I guess not." Thomas became uneasy. "It comes down to one of three possibilities. Bohica has either been moved, hidden, or destroyed. We haven't found any indications of destruction. We've pretty much given up on that idea. Hiding it seems possible to most of us, although we don't know how. A few believe that it's been moved, but nobody gives that theory much consideration. I've been told that the variations in orbits of the other planets and the tests we've run, suggest it's not there. And just who am I addressing?"

The Green lizard looked at Thomas. His stare lingered, frozen in time. Yellow-green globs dripped down the polished skin of his forearm. Finally, he said, "I think your possibilities are correct, but why did you give up on the planetary destruction?"

"What are you talking about? As I said, we didn't find any evidence." Thomas' mind quickly went through the information given him by the crew of the *Gold Rat*. "The geological monitoring stations we set up earlier gave no warning of instability. There was nothing that would indicate a natural disaster. And you must admit that it's hard to think of someone annihilating an entire world. Now please answer my question. Who are you?"

"I have heard about what you have done to your mother planet." The arrogance in the Green lizard's tone was unmistakable.

"It's not that bad," Thomas replied quickly, wondering what exaggerations he had heard.

The reptile pointed his unsoiled claw at the second table from them. "See those soldiers? Their glory is based on a lifeless rock, a chunk of mass that once held an abundance of life."

"I know the story," said Thomas.

The three similarly dressed and noisy reptiles had pronounced light-brown scales, and a hard spinal ridge running from nose to tail.

They had a disagreement with a species of two-meter-high praying mantis-like insects. The dispute centered around food. The sharp tooth's reptiles were hungry, and the insects didn't want to be food. It took half a rotation around the star for the lizards to turn the lush green environment of that world into a useless lump in space. The last Thomas heard they were still hungry.

His companion continued, "Are you willing to admit that it is at least possible for Bohica to be destroyed?"

"Perhaps, but no energy patterns that suggest a deliberate act were detected."

"What wavelengths and durations were you checking?"

"I'm sure we checked all the right energy ranges that could cause such a massive effect. It must be really obvious." Thomas could feel his temper building, what his wife had called a slow burn.

"I think I'm beginning to understand," said the Green lizard, as if to someone else, during another long stare. "Perhaps you're looking in the wrong place. Perhaps it takes less time than you can imagine. Perhaps a planet can be disposed of, in. . . .," he held up all eight of his digits, "converted into your measure, less then sixty-four femto-seconds." His mood had changed. The polite conversation turned very blunt.

"Did you say femto-seconds?" Realizing the period mentioned would be instantaneous, Thomas could only mutter, "That's impossible."

"Impossible? Do humans believe that things are not possible?"

"All right. As technically inconceivable as it may be, let's say Bohica is obliterated. Who did it? We got permission from every system in the surrounding sectors before we colonized. Nobody wanted Bohica. It's too close to the environmental edge for the species in the area. Yet we could make it suitable for us. Why would someone destroy it?" Thomas started to get angry.

The Green reptile licked the last bit of goo off his claw with his tongue now yellow-green stained, stood up, picked up the bowl, and gave Thomas another stare. "Maybe someone didn't want you there," the lizard said.

"Who are you?" Thomas did everything he could to keep from yelling.

"An interested party." The lizard turned and casually walked out of the bar.

Thomas sat there, struggling to regain his composure. He didn't understand how this creature could so easily infuriate him. He had dealt with more arrogant and righteous aliens in his career as a negotiator. Handling them was easy, with no personal involvement to crowd his mind.

Thomas walked out of the bar of Many Welcomes and into the open corridor to where George waited.

"I hope the meeting went well," said the young man sitting in the vehicle.

"Let's go."

Thomas couldn't stop thinking about what that smooth-skinned reptile had said. Their conversation was burning into his brain. That lizard had lost patience talking to Thomas and that upset him even more. After all, humans were hurt here. His people. Then the horrible reality sank in. That slime sucking lizard told him Bohica had been not moved, not hidden and destroyed. The trip back would bring no joy.

"I have made arrangements for you to rest here for . . ."

"No. Back to the ship. Now." Thomas didn't want anything to divert his mind from what had to be done at that moment.

Approaching the parking bay of the *Monkey's Fist*, Thomas saw Kert and Keil walking across the staging floor.

"How did it go, Thomas? We were going to grab a bite to eat. Would you like to join us?" Kert asked.

"No. We must leave immediately." He got out of the vehicle and walked toward the *Monkey's Fist*.

"Extraordinary happenings," Keil said to Kert

"Mr. McCormick," George yelled after him.

Thomas turned.

"What happened to Bohica?"

"I don't know."

Thomas had no recollection of what he did after that. He didn't remember thanking George, getting into the ship or the transition into space. His body felt as numb as his mind as his oath to Angelica's safety crumbled. He had never felt like such a failure. The resounding thump on the hull returned him to the events of the moment.

"I need to talk to the *Gold Rat.*"

"Sure." Kile made the connection. Soon both Ned and Taffa-Lee were on the monitor listening to Thomas' recount of his meeting. They didn't ask questions until Thomas had finished.

"Are you sure he said less than sixty-four femto-seconds?" Taffa-Lee asked.

"Yes. He made a point of it. Why?"

"It's an extremely small measure of time. I'm not sure any of our equipment can measure anything that quick. And if we can't measure it, then how could it happen? It doesn't sound possible. I'll talk to Rusty about our capabilities. He knows these systems better than anyone and may have some ideas. But to be honest with you, Thomas, I'm not hopeful." Her pained expression matched her words.

"If this is true," Ned interjected, "it would confirm a hostile move against humans in this region, putting us all in danger. We must be very careful. We're not even sure who is responsible. The Tri-Bah had the most opportunity but is the least logical group. How convinced are you of this new player's involvement?"

"I'm not sure." He said he was an interested party. "Could be Fire Lizards or another species. It could be a group within one of the races, depending on their social economic structure. For that matter, he could have been some crazy lizard that walked in off the thorough path. That's why it's important to verify this information. We must be sure."

"We agree," Taffa-Lee said.

"Good. I'll turn you over to Keil. If possible, you two can work out a location where we can go back in time to take another set of readings and verify this once and for all."

"I'm not sure we can even take readings fast enough to make this measurement."

"What if we sped the ship up. The image might come in slower." When Thomas said that he knew he was outside his area of expertise.

"I'm sorry that won't work."

"Work it out as best you can."

"But what if we can't?" Taffa-Lees' voice was strained.

"I'm sure you'll think of something. There must be a way. I think that the lizards had expected us to figure it out already. Here's Keil."

Thomas went back to the bunk where he had spent most of his time in the small ship. He didn't know how long it would take to reach the rendezvous point with the *Gold Rat*, and he didn't care. He felt defeated and drained. His only hope was to confirm that Bohica had been purposefully destroyed, make his report to Rodriguez, and go home. He needed Charm to hold.

CHAPTER 12

Victor paced behind the pilot's chair. There wasn't that much room, but he could pull off that illusion anyway.

"Here we go," the pilot said. She made an adjustment to the controls as they moved out of Q-space and into the real universe. "This can't be right."

"What is it?" Victor leaned forward to study the instruments.

"I know I plotted the course correctly. It just doesn't look like we're in the right system."

The stress in her voice told Victor what he needed to know. The rumors and vague reports were all true. Thomas' trail had not grown cold. His excitement to push forward spun inside him.

But he remained calm. He wanted to reassure Yang that her piloting was fine.

"What makes you think we're not in the right place?"

"There should be a gravity well here," she said, pointing to a display. "Instead, there are a lot of ships in that area."

"It's okay. We're in the right place, but Bohica is gone."

"How can that be?"

He put his hand on her shoulder to reassure her. "That's why we came. Now, let's see if we can find Thomas' ship."

After several inquiries Victor finally got in contact with the ship that appeared to be in charge. A dark-faced woman with a smooth rich voice greeted him on the screen.

"Namaste. My name is Safrona-Lu, Communications Officer of the escort, *Assegai*. We are advising all ships that a Union investigation is underway, and we have no information to give out at this time.

There is no reason to stay in this system and we suggest that you continue on to, your destination."

"Greetings to you." Victor wondered how many times she had repeated her message. Her tone droned lifelessly. "I'm looking for Thomas McCormick. I believe he is on the *Gold Rat*. Can you help me find him?"

"Who are you and what is this concerning?" Her voice snapped to life.

Victor didn't want to play bureaucratic tag, especially with a skilled secretary. He must cut through the polite rhetoric.

"My name is . . .," he hesitated while thinking quickly. "Wiseman, Victor Wiseman. I have recently been appointed as Vice Representative to the Union by the Great Shono Toroid. I have orders to contact Representative McCormick on an urgent and confidential matter of Union business. I must see him immediately."

"One moment."

Victor knew what she was up to and anticipated her response.

"It shows someone else as Representative of the Shono Toroid."

"As I said, I have just been appointed. Not all the data bases have been updated. And if you know anything about the political stability of Shono, I could be recalled tomorrow. But today I must talk with McCormick."

"He's not here. He is on the *Gold Rat* and has moved away from the system to make some measurements. Perhaps you can wait until they return or talk with him ship to ship."

"No. That won't do. I need to stand before him as soon as possible." Victor put enough edge and tension in his voice to express his urgency. He didn't want to frighten or alarm Safrona-Lu. The last thing he wanted was to raise suspicions.

"I'm going to give you the location of the *Gold Rat*. However, Representative McCormick is not there. I just found out he is in route and will transfer to the *Gold Rat* before you arrive."

Victor could feel the hesitation and hear the reluctance in her voice. He didn't care. He would finally meet with Thomas McCormick.

*   *   *

"Wake up," said Kert.

Thomas found himself still in the bunk and had fallen asleep. He shook his head shaking off a bad 'First Day of School' dream. But instead of looking for his classroom, he was looking for Bohica. No one knew where it was, and Angelica was missing.

"Thomas, would you like something to eat?"

"I'm not really hungry." Looking at Kert, he knew he had overslept. "How long before we meet up with the *Gold Rat?*"

"About an hour. That's why I woke you."

"Thank you. I'm all right for now. Maybe I'll have something later." Despite the rest, he felt tired, defeated and as depressed as before.

By the time they popped into normal space, he had eaten and felt almost human. The *Gold Rat* contacted them first. They were on station and ready to observe the event. As they hooked up, Thomas gathered the few items he had brought. He made his way thru the narrow passageway between the two ships and saw the smiling face of Lee-Hope.

"Did you have a pleasant trip, Mr. McCormick?" She asked in her business voice.

"No." He snapped, and then softened it with, "Not really." There was no reason to take it out on her.

"I'm sorry to hear that." She took his bag and disappeared into the ship.

Thomas needed to find a person he could relate to and talk with about his troubled thoughts. The crew of the *Gold Rat* may not have been the best choice, but it was all he had. And they were waiting for him. He slid into the bench seat at the table. Only Rusty was missing.

"I thought you might like some tea," Martha-Key said, filling a cup in front of him.

"Thank you." He took a long drink. "It feels good."

Rusty appeared from a hole under a console. He climbed out and took a seat at the table next to Martha-Key.

"Tell Thomas what you have been up to?" Taffa-Lee asked.

"Do you know anything about the configuration of cascading trigger buffers?"

Thomas had no answer.

"I didn't think so." Rusty continued. "What I did is to set up the equipment to stretch out the time in the data storage by triggering them faster. This will let us play it back and see the results of very fast events. We should be able to see down to the ten or twenty femtosecond ranges."

"Unfortunately, the new configuration will not let us take a full set of readings," Taffa-Lee added. "We narrowed it down to three: photon, graviton and X-ray. These should give us the best results. However, the resolution is poor if your information is correct."

"Will we actually get to see it happen?" Asked Thomas.

"No. The optical system can't be set up that way. We will only record the intensity of the light as the planet changes."

Thomas could see Taffa-Lee look at his eyes. Could she see how he felt? His pain must be visible. Defeat etched lines into his face. "They destroyed Bohica," he said, as if that was what they were talking about.

"We know."

"All those people are gone. Angelica and her husband. I don't understand." Using the table for support, Thomas buried his head in his hands. He couldn't contain his pent-up frustration any longer.

"We knew that was a possibility," explained Taffa-Lee. "Why don't you go freshen up. We'll consider the consequences later. The event happens in 38 minutes. And we have a lot of equipment checking to do. We'll call you when it's time."

Splashing water in his face helped but didn't wash away his feelings. It reminded him of what Lee-Hope said, 'Where there's no sense, there's no feeling.' Now, he not only needed an answer, but also resolution. Someone did this. They may have had a reason, but it wasn't known. Thomas hoped they would receive the consequence of their actions. But the human race was in no position to dictate terms.

The recognizable knock of Lee-Hope startled him. Thomas once again went to the Operations center and stared into a monitor waiting for the unseen magician to perform his disappearing trick.

Then it appeared - an indication, a squiggle, a blip.

"Look at that. It measures fifty femto-seconds and is bigger than a sun," Rusty said.

"Impossible!" Taffa-Lee said.

Rusty checked his settings and played back the sweep. He got the same results.

"It's conclusive, Thomas. Someone had generated enough energy, induced it into the planet, transformed all the matter into energy, and vented the residue in such a way as not to disturb the surrounding system or leave a trace," Ned explained. "All this in fifty millionths of a billionth of a second,"

His depressed state drove him to the solitude of his cabin. In the dark he mentally composed a communique to the publishers of Whitman's Catalog, suggesting an addition to the definition of intra species intelligence. We should not only measure the magnitude of transformation that can be accomplished by a species, but also how quickly it could be done. Thomas had changed his mind on the notion of what was impossible. The truth would be hard to live with.

"Thomas," came a cry from the hallway. He opened his door and found a very excited Martha-Key.

"A ship is approaching. Vice Representative Victor Wiseman from the Shono Toroid wants to come aboard and talk with you."

"There's another Rep out here?" Thomas asked desperately.

Taffa-Lee joined them. "Can you vouch for him? We feel really uncomfortable about letting strangers onboard."

"Well, I've never heard of him, but that doesn't mean he's not a Representative."

Taffa-Lee relayed the story to Thomas about Wiseman's recent appointment as a Representative, his urgent Union business with Thomas and a need for a face-to-face talk.

Inside Thomas felt relief flush over him. He no longer had to carry the burden all by himself. Another Rep meant they could do more, see more and be in two places at the same time. But most important, it was another person to talk with about this depressing mystery.

"So, what do we do?" Taffa-Lee was waiting for an answer.

"Let's talk with him and find out what he knows."

"Are you sure, Thomas?"

"I don't think we have much of a choice."

The two ships docked, and Thomas and the two co-captains gathered to greet the new Representative. Since he wasn't a paying customer, Lee-Hope didn't meet him at the airlock. Instead, she waited in Operations with the others.

Through the short passageway from the airlock came a figure in black and white de-comp armor. The heavily armed person stepped aside, and another entered the ship. They had one hand on an energy weapon, a disrupter strapped to their backs and the biggest kanashimi knife Thomas had ever seen. Apparently, it was a trench knife with sharp points protruding from the finger guards.

Lee-Hope's mother and father quickly moved back toward the stairs. Heightened alarm and panic dominated the emotion that ran through each of them.

Ned removed his blade, a brave act. Thomas wasn't a weapons or military expert, but he knew that a one-second blast from that disrupter could turn the *Gold Rat* inside out.

Chapter 13

"Those mammals are stupid," the Green lizard growled, as he spun around. His heavy black tunic tried to catch up with his movements. The skin on his head shone like polished rock. "They don't have the understanding to be out here. They should stay in their holes and chew rocks."

"The Tri-Bah believes that we can learn from all species," the Group Master said, wishing this annoyance would go away. He didn't like siding with the other creatures. But since the Green lizard had returned from the meeting with the humans he had been agitated. The Group Master didn't care.

"That is political rhetoric," said the Green lizard. "If your kind truly believed those words, this would never have been allowed to happen. The fact is its now history. And therefore, these humans are of no importance to you. They are certainly worthless to me. So let them scurry around all they want. You make your report and we'll be done with this."

Nothing would make the Group Master happier than to leave these problems behind and set the Envoy adrift. Everything had gotten more complicated and has not turned out as everyone had predicted.

"I have other matters to consider. The stability of my region depends on the smooth interaction of many species." The Group Master stepped closer and looked the Envoy in the face. "For that reason, we must be careful to dissipate all their anger and mistrust. The humans have never shown themselves as a threat but could stir up some of the others. The agitation could be an annoyance."

"I don't care. The demonstration is over. If you want to herd these creatures around space that is fine with me. But our leaders have more important business to deal with."

"We are drifting far from the subject." The Group Master wished he could send this raving lizard on his way, but his orders didn't permit that. "I just want to know if they understand that there is nothing more for them to do, and they need to leave."

"I put it in very clear terms to that creature I met with. Whether or not that was understood and communicated to the rest of them, I have no idea. You may have to go there and shoo them away." The Green lizard stared at the Group Master and made little hand movements as if you would to insects or children.

The Group Master had enough. He turned and left the room.

*　　*　　*

The first intruder on the *Gold Rat* put up a hand, the palm forward. This gesture was simple, *stop, everything will be all right.* This didn't ease their fears. The other menacing figure quickly surveyed the rest of the ship. By the time they got back together, an older man with a soft gray beard had joined them.

"Thomas McCormick?" he asked, stepping forward. "I'm Victor Wiseman. I have looked forward to meeting you." His eyes were bright and his handshake firm.

Thomas gestured to the two armed figures. "What the hell is the meaning of all of this?"

"What gives you the right to bring weapons aboard my ship?" Ned added.

"These are just my bodyguards. They insist on all the dramatic precautions. I apologize for any inconvenience or distress." His smile was sincere and friendly. "They are Yen and Yang."

Thomas realized the black and white scheme on the de-comp armor had a random pattern and the opposite configuration on the other figure.

"The Union gave you bodyguards?" Thomas felt less valuable and more second class.

"No, they didn't. These are my personal bodyguards."

As greetings were given all around, the two ominous figures returned to the other ship. Victor's curiosity burst forth in the form of many questions about Bohica and what Thomas had been doing.

"Wait a minute," Taffa-Lee said. "How do we know that you are a Representative?" She didn't seem ready to give up the intrusion onto her ship.

"I'm sorry. The only proof are public records. Unfortunately, the bureaucracy of the Shono Toroid and the Union are such that it will be days before my name shows up on any official data bases. I would be surprised if you could find your name, Thomas. You haven't been a Rep that long."

"What do we do?" Taffa-Lee asked, turning to Thomas.

"Well, Thomas, I could give you the secret handshake," Victor said with a grin.

"What secret handshake?"

"I'm just kidding. I'll make a deal with you. You tell me everything you know, and I'll tell you everything I know."

"Perhaps." Thomas didn't feel he had much of a choice. He needed all the help he could get and nobody else had volunteered.

Victor, Thomas, Taffa-Lee and Rusty sat down at the table and went over everything they had done in the last twelve days. Victor listened intently and only interrupted now and then with specific questions; surprisingly, some of them technically good.

When Thomas relayed his encounter with the Green lizard, Victor and his questions became more intense. Thomas only wished he had those answers to share.

When Victor had gotten caught up to date, Martha-Key joined them. "I've analyzed the new data," she said. "The gravitational data showed us what happened."

"Was that the little blip on the screen we saw?" Thomas asked.

"Yes. I now understand why Bohica's destruction occurred so quickly. The theory is called Temporal Columnation."

"What?"

"A better name might be Time Stacking."

"Not better enough. I still don't understand." Thomas shook his head.

"It's like this." Martha-Key placed her hands in front of her, palms facing each other as if to measure something. "The entire event of blowing up the planet, which may take anywhere from a few minutes to a year, is integrated into an infinite number of temporal slices." She motioned with one hand like a knife chopping up a vegetable. "Each slice is then displaced back in time, to the start of the event, so that it appears to happen all at once." She brought both of her hands together. "The fifty femto-seconds we observed were nothing more than a registration error of the slices stacked on top of each other. The end of the event may occur at four femto-seconds and the beginning of the event could be at the fortieth."

"So, what you're saying is that Bohica's destruction may not have taken an instant, but just looked like it did?" Thomas asked, excited about the revelation, and the possibility that it may not be as hard a thing to do as he first thought.

"Yes," Martha-Key answered.

"What's the difference?" Victor asked.

"I guess there isn't any." Thomas realized what he had said. "But wouldn't all that activity at one point in time cause some temporal distortion, or something? Sustaining the process might be difficult."

"Maybe not, if it's localized," said Martha-Key. "Perhaps it's more efficient to blow up a planet because it happens all at once. Sort of like a chain reaction."

"How is this done? How do you stack time?" Asked Victor.

"We don't know," she said.

"That still doesn't explain how it was destroyed," Thomas said.

"Maybe that's exactly how it was done." Victor had a look of enlightenment. "If you move an object back in time a femto-second, that object is occupying the same space twice."

"So?" Thomas was again very confused.

"Don't you see?" Rusty said with excitement in his voice. "You would have two planets. Twice the mass would take up the same room. The object would crumble and burst. If you, did it a hundred thousand times, you would have a hundred thousand times Bohica's mass." Rusty quickly moved to a terminal and brought up one of the graphs from a sensor. "See this spike? It's a gravity wave at the time of the disappearance. It's huge. Hundreds of thousands of Bohicas occupied the same point in space."

"That's what blew up Bohica," Taffa-Lee said, just above a whisper. She had been quiet but listening over their shoulders.

"Just moving it back in time?" Thomas Asked, his mind reeling.

"It's more than that." Rusty continued. "We have all been looking for an indication of the energy used to destroy Bohica. Something simple, like a large disrupter to blow it up. But that's not the case. Bohica was folded on top of itself thousands of times and collapsed from the sheer weight."

Thomas felt the idea sink in. He had been lost trying to understand the technical information. Rusty was finally getting through. Even Thomas could recognize the importance of these revelations.

"Well then," Thomas said, more relaxed. "Where are the remains of a hundred thousand Bohicas? Are they scattered throughout the system? Would it have turned into a sun or black hole?"

"I don't think that would happen." Victor said, his eyes lost in the question.

"You're right," Martha-key said. "When the machinery stops slicing up time and stacking them, everything would proceed forward normally. All the Bohicas, or should I say, the rubble of Bohica would sort itself out until only the rubble of one planet remains."

Ned leaned closer to the table. "Those four ships we saw diving toward Bohica before it disappeared must have carried the equipment to do this."

"But they disappeared also," Thomas said.

"You're right. And those were large ships. This was a very expensive magic trick. Are you saying they were destroyed also?" Asked Ned.

"Yes."

"Then where is the debris from the one Bohica?" Thomas asked the question calmly, though his heart sank when he thought of Angelica.

"We don't know," Taffa-Lee said, after searching the faces of her crew. "I'm not sure what form Bohica would take. Nothing bigger than grains of sand, perhaps dust or even plasma. We're dealing with a different kind of physics. The *Gold Rat* is not equipped to survey these kinds of temporal mechanics."

Thomas knew they wouldn't have that answer. This whole trip had turned up question after question and no answers.

"Okay, make sure your ideas get in the report," Thomas said, again depressed.

"But who did it?" The clear small voice of Lee-Hope asked. The rest of them didn't even see her come into the room.

"We don't know, sweetheart," Taffa-Lee said, more as a concerned mother than a scientist.

"I keep coming up with three choices," Rusty said. "The Fire Lizards, Surriens or that new lizard you found."

"I agree," Victor added, as he stroked his beard. "Unless there is a totally random wild card at work that we don't know about."

Thomas stood and stepped to the center of the room. His mind had gotten sluggish. He had been at this for too long. He put his palms on the ceiling of the Operations room and stretched. Lowering his arms, he could feel blood rush through every cubic centimeter of his body.

Thomas could see everyone from where he stood. "If the Surriens are responsible, we would have to handle it. I don't believe the Fire Lizards would get involved. We leased Bohica from them. They didn't want it. Also, the Surriens are no threat to them, and they are well outside the Tri-Bah territories."

"That seems reasonable," Victor said.

Ned agreed.

"If the Green lizards, did it," Thomas continued, "I think the Fire lizards would get involved. If for no other reason than to make sure they were no threat."

"And If they are not," Ned added, "it's still up to us."

"That's right." Thomas realized he had been slowly pacing. "That leaves us with the unlikely Fire Lizards."

"Why is the Tri-Bah so unlikely?" Lee-Hope asked.

"Most species feel lucky to live under the shadow of their empire. They bring a degree of protection to a region. The Fire Lizards won't tolerate marauders or any disruption to the trade routes. They are fair and honest with most business dealings." Thomas began to sound like a teacher.

"However," Victor added, "if there is something they want, they don't mind pushing their weight around."

"I agree with that," said Taffa-Lee. "And we still don't have an answer as to who did this."

After that, no one had much to add.

Thomas realized that he had questions for someone else. "So, Victor, what brings you out here, so far from the Shono Toroid?"

"I had business on Hector. That's where I found out about my appointment as Vice Rep."

"If I remember correctly, Shono is a planet with an asteroid ring. A gas giant?"

"It's a small gas planet with an asteroid ring cloud. A very rare variety."

"How many mines are operational?" Thomas carefully studied the old man's face.

"Eighteen. But we're opening a new one almost every year."

"Business aside, why are you here checking up on Bohica?"

"To see what you are up to. Make my own assessment of the potential threats. And to encourage you to keep up the good work." Victor's smile seemed a little too big.

"Did Director Rodriguez send you?"

"Not directly."

"Are you checking up on me? Does he not trust me or think I can't handle this investigation?" Thomas realized that his abilities might have been in question. He felt uneasy enough in the middle of this chaos without someone looking over his shoulder.

"No, not at all. You continue with your investigation and your job. I'm not here to interfere with that. I have my own information to gather. That's all."

Thomas felt a little better, but he still had questions. "What are you looking for?"

"I'm here for an overview and to help out. Please accept that for what it is."

Victor had seemed honest enough. His smile was a little too friendly, but Thomas would accept that for now. He was weary. Victor said he would take his own ship back to Bohica and left. Thomas made his way to his tiny cabin desperate for sleep.

His mind could not let go of what their investigation had found. He had hoped that the baffling disappearance would be easy to explain. It wasn't. Thomas didn't want to believe what had happened to Angelica. She had come here to find a new home, to make a place for herself among the stars, and all that other poetic rot. Bohica was a worthless rock, but it was humanity's worthless rock. Instead of her finding a great future, Thomas had found a blip, a burning cross. *Go away. You're not wanted here.*

CHAPTER 14

Victor stepped back onto his ship and activated the air lock seal that closed behind him. "Let's get out of here," he said to Yang.

"Where are we going?" She asked as she sat in the pilot's chair.

"Back to Bohica."

"You mean, back to where it was?"

"Yes, back to the system."

"Do they suspect anything?" Yen asked.

"No. Thomas is too gullible and trusting. He may learn a tough lesson before this is over." Victor made his way back to his small cabin, sat cross-legged on the soft bunk, took the red cloth off his book and opened it. But his mind wandered about the discussion with the crew of the *Gold Rat* and not the pages of his honored book.

Thomas had accepted the story about Victor being a Rep. That deception could not last long. Soon Victor would have to finish his work, or he would have to tell Thomas the truth. At this point both outcomes seemed unknown.

The passage jumped out at him.

> *The difficulty of tactical maneuvering consists in turning the devious into the direct, and misfortune into gain.*

Bohica might never be found.

*   *   *

The Group Master walked down the long narrow hall that led to the Operations Center at the heart of his flagship, the *Inner Stone*. Every step boomed and echoed as he became more upset. His mission had turned to quick-mud. It started out so simple and became sticky at every node and juncture. And it remained his responsibility to resolve these issues and return the surrounding sector back to normal. He hated to be given a job he had no control over.

By the time he reached the Operations Center his anger made him feel like a lizard on fire. He slammed the door open and stomped inside. Many of the crew at terminals around the room glanced at him and then nervously looked away.

"Sub Group Commander," he yelled, not trying to control himself. It felt good to let go, to reassert his leadership and authority.

"Yes, Sir." The tall second in command approached the Group Master and stood in defiance of the mood.

The Group Master had seen this look before. His Second stood, prepared to defend his command and warfighters from whatever wrong they had done.

"Not to worry, Second," he said in a lowered voice, "The ship has performed well." In times like these he truly valued his officers and their loyalty to the crew.

"Thank you, Master."

"Prepare to move the fleet," he said, the edgy loud volume returning to his voice. "Make for the Bohica system as soon as we're ready."

"Yes, Group Master." The Sub Group Commander turned away to bark orders at those sitting on the floor at the terminals around the room.

As he walked out of the Operations Center, the Group Master stopped. "I want to make a polar approach to the system, and don't pop into normal space too close. I don't want to spook the animals."

*　　*　　*

The trip back to Bohica had been long and slow for Thomas. He couldn't bring himself to talk with Rodriguez. Not yet. He really wanted to go home. They would have, except that Safona-Lu on the *Assegai* had told them that a lot more ships have entered the Bohica system. It would be his responsibility to send them away. He entertained the idea to try and talk Victor into it, but his success in doing that seemed unlikely.

The *Gold Rat* began to shutter. Thomas sat up in his bunk disturbed by the vibration. With the familiar, but louder pop on the hull, the ship slipped smoothly back to normal space. He bolted out of his small cabin and made his way toward the Operations room.

"What the hell was that?" Thomas asked, as he entered.

"We're not sure," Taffa-Lee answered. "We had some kind of cavitation just before popping back into normal-space."

"All systems are okay," Ned shouted from the pilot's position above them in the forward section of the ship.

"Put us in touch with Wiseman," Thomas said to Martha-key. "Let's find out if he had any problems."

Victor's worried face stared back through the terminal at Thomas. "No. We didn't experience any problems. You might run maintenance on your interface stabilization."

"Ned has already thought of that. He's working on that now," said Thomas.

Taffa-Lee walked up to Thomas. "We can't find anything that would cause that," she said.

"Did you hear that?" Thomas asked.

"Yes."

"I just wanted to check with you." Thomas keyed off the terminal.

Everyone seemed to be relieved. Thomas debated if he should get a cup of tea or go back and lay down. His answer came quickly.

"There must be more than thirty ships in the area," Martha-key said. She turned around and looked up at Thomas. "They want to talk to you."

"Why?" Thomas asked.

"Because you're in charge."

"I understand that. I mean, why do they feel a need to talk to me and what do they want to talk about? Never mind. I'll see what they want." Thomas resigned himself to a long stretch in front of a terminal. "First I'm getting some tea."

After five hours, Thomas had enough. If he heard, "Is there anything we can do to help," one more time he would scream. It seemed a good gesture, especially from the alien ships. But there was nothing left to do, and no one left to save.

Rest was what he needed. But he didn't find it in his bunk. Too many conversations of people and aliens wanting to help ran through his mind. He also had the report to give to Rodriguez. That nightmare couldn't be forgotten.

Neither sleep, rest nor comfort came to Thomas in the dark, only a restless desire for what he couldn't possess. He made his way forward to get something to drink. He wondered if Ned had a bottle of hard stuff tucked away. He found Martha-Key and Lee-Hope at the table. It looked like school was in session.

"Hello," said Thomas. "I hope I'm not disturbing you."

"Not at all, Thomas. In fact, I think we're ready for a break," Martha-Key said.

"We're doing math and it's really hard," said Lee-Hope

"It wasn't my favorite either," Thomas said, pouring himself a cup of tea and sitting down. "What kind are you learning this time?"

"Algebra."

"It's good for you."

"You had a message a while ago," Martha-Key said, "from a Surrien priest. He sounded very upset with you."

"What did I do this time?"

"I'm not sure. But I did get the impression that he wanted to kick your butt."

"Really?"

"Yes. I put the file in your queue so you can look at it whenever you're ready. I didn't wake you because I thought you needed the rest."

"Thanks, I did."

"Mr. McCormick," said Martha-Key. "A question came up about mining while we were doing History. I was wondering if you could explain the difference between type-one, two and three mining operations."

"Sure. Type-one is like what we were doing on Tuska. Breathable atmosphere, everyone lived above ground, and no special environmental requirements. The mining and refining are all done outside, from the surface down. This is by far the best way to do mining or do anything. Unfortunately, anyone can do that kind of mining. Even the locals. They don't need humans and therefore we're out of a job in most Type-ones."

Lee-Hope remained attentive.

"A type-two operation is done in a hostile environment. Special shelters are built and/or protective equipment is required. This is the most expensive type of mining. Humans don't like to do it, but we have. It depends on the hostility of the environment. Some are not as bad as others."

"Type-three," Thomas continued, "is like what they are doing on Bohica. It has no atmosphere and it's just a large rock." Thomas stopped. What he said sank in. The pain returned along with the despair and something new, shame for himself making mistakes and acting so awkwardly in front of others. "I mean that it was a large rock." He forced a smile and fought to regain his composure.

"Anyway, the entire operation was done underground. You can live, work, mine, and do the refining in a controlled environment. This is what humans are good at."

"It's too bad we can't do more type-one mining," Lee-Hope said, with a naive childish yearning that fit her age.

"Well, . . ." An unpleasant sound from a terminal cut Thomas off.

Martha-Key responded to the pulsating noise. She displayed data, but Thomas had no understanding of what it meant.

"What's happening?" Thomas asked, with Ned and Taffa-Lee running into the room. Rusty followed.

"It's a small passenger runabout. The distress signal is coming through the frogging repeaters. There, it just popped into normal space." Martha-Key changed the display.

The image of a ship appeared slowly moving across the screen. Clear evident damage could be seen around the front of the craft. Out gassing and leaks were also visible. Several ships moved in to give support.

Thomas wondered if Rodriguez's warning at the beginning of his journey was true. Could marauders have caused the damage on the runabout? Could the rest of the ships defend themselves, the group or the system?

Chapter 15

"It doesn't look like weapons damage," Taffa-Lee said.

"It could have been a rail gun canister," Rusty added. "They can do damage like that."

Ned sat at another terminal. He pulled up different data.

"See if you can contact that ore freighter," Ned told Martha-Key. "It looks like it's the closest one and will get there first."

After persistent work she made contact.

"This is Captain Patel of the freighter *Wide River*," a labored voice replied. "We have managed to identify eight survivors held up in the life pods and three dead. The hull has many small to medium-size breaches at the nose of the runabout. They might have collided with something."

Thomas strained his ears to hear the clear sound coming from the terminal. He found himself breathing heavily and his muscles tense.

"Captain, do you have any information about other craft in the area? Were they attacked?"

"We have no indication of another ship. We are about to retrieve the crew. When we have them safely aboard, we'll contact you. Out."

"I guess all we can do is wait," Taffa-Lee said. She and Lee-Hope went off to put together a meal. Thomas tried to look patient and professional. Inside he churned with worry about possible attacks on all the ships.

What if this was some kind of elaborate hoax to lure ships into a group and attack them while they were off guard? Thomas couldn't contain his suspicions.

"Rusty," Thomas said, "do you think this could be a kind of trap?"

"What do you mean?"

"Don't you think it's very convenient to have all these ships gathered in one place? Think about it. A group of marauders could swoop in here and really hit pay dirt."

"I don't think that is very likely." Rusty leaned back in his chair and stretched his long arms over his head

"Why?"

"Many of these ships are armed and several are designed for escort service. Also, there's safety in numbers. It wouldn't make sense to do that."

"Maybe you're right."

"*Gold Rat*, this is the *Monkey's Fist*," the voice said, coming from Martha-Key's terminal. "Two heavily armed vessels have entered the system and are moving toward your position."

"Thank you, *Monkey's Fist*," she replied. "Stay on your toes."

Thomas usually enjoyed being right. This time he felt sick in his stomach.

Everyone huddled around the monitors. Thomas thought about how familiar this had become. This time the crew of the *Gold Rat* watched two heavily armed ships slowly approach. The two unknown vessels didn't take a stationary position like all the other ships. Nor were they in a hurry or acting timid in any way. As Martha-Key worked to pick up a transponder code, they moved directly for the *Gold Rat*.

"Should we think about moving or getting out of here?" Thomas felt the walls closing in.

"Not just yet." Taffa-Lee put her hand on his shoulder.

"There it is," Martha-Key said. "It's the *Black Watch* and the *Black Knight*."

"That's Ivan Black," Taffa-Lee said, turning and looking at Thomas.

"No." Dread followed a cold shiver as Thomas tried to think. "We've got to do something."

"What?" Ned asked.

"He's a marauder. We have to warn the other ships and get out of here."

"Nonsense. Relax, Thomas, he's our business partner. We've been expecting them."

Now it was Thomas' turn to say, "What?" He then remembered the late-night conversation with Martha-Key on how the *Gold Rat* was a partnership. How could these people that he had grown to trust and respect, be involved with a criminal type like Ivan Black? "Director Rodriguez said that Black was a marauder and might be involved with Bohica's disappearance."

"Ridiculous," Ned said.

"Rodriguez doesn't know his ass from a mineshaft," Rusty added.

After the *Black Watch* and *Gold Rat* docked, Thomas observed a flurry of hugs, women laughing, men smiling and all the chatter of a family reunion. After many greetings and handshakes, Thomas found himself in front of a tall man with long tied-back gray hair and a deeply wrinkled face. His black jumpsuit with gray trim seemed to be the standard uniform for that crew.

"So, you're Thomas McCormick, the Union Representative," he said, giving him a firm handshake.

"And you're the infamous Ivan Black." Thomas felt relieved when that brought a smile to the hard face.

Black turned to Ned with a somber expression. "So, where's Bohica?"

"We don't know. But we would like to show you what we've learned," Taffa-Lee said.

"Stop." Thomas couldn't believe what he was hearing. "This information belongs to the Union. You are under contract to relinquish this data to only a Union Representative." Thomas couldn't understand what happened to these people.

"It's all right, Thomas." Ned's voice tried to sooth him.

"No, it's not."

"Yes, it is," said Ivan, his expression softened. "Because Ned and I are partners, we are both bound under the same contract. It's not going anywhere."

Thomas felt helpless in a world out of control. Too many people were learning the truth. Rodriguez's warning to tell no one echoed in his mind. What was he to do? If he had trusted the crew of the *Gold Rat*, he would have to do the same for Ivan Black and Thomas wasn't a lawyer enough to do otherwise.

Thomas saw the glowing face of Lee-Hope gazing up at them.

"Where's Daniel?" She asked with a smile.

"He can't make it this time. He's on the *Black Wolf*, escorting a convoy down spin from Homestead. My you've grown as much as he has and getting as pretty as your mom."

Lee-Hope forced another smile, but Thomas could see her disappointment.

"I've got Captain Patel of the *Wide River* back on," Martha-Key said. "They have finished recovering the bodies and survivors."

"Would you see if I could talk to one of the crew," Thomas asked? "The captain would be best."

After some confusing movement a man set in front of the terminal to talk with Thomas. He had a blanket draped over his shoulders and bandages on his left hand. He looked cold and in shock.

"I'm sorry. Our captain is dead. I'm the engineer." His voice contained no emotion, just the flat tone of stress and weariness.

"That's all right. I need to know if there was another ship. Were you attacked?"

"No. We were getting ready to enter normal space. Everything seemed fine. Then the collision alarm sounded. It caught us off guard. There wasn't much we could do."

"Can you describe what it was like? Was it a single object?"

The injured man took his time. As he thought, he massaged his forehead. "Have you ever heard the rain? I did once on Ichorous. It was beautiful like that. It echoed through the hull, and yet at the same time terrifying."

"There are some that think it could have been a canister round from a rail gun. What do you think?"

"I thought of that. It's a possibility, but I don't know."

"Thomas," Ivan said, as he leaned closer, "ask him if there was any burst of static from communications. Sometimes the frogging repeaters pick up an RF pulse from the rail gun in Q- space."

"Frogging Repeater," Martha-Key said, as if she had forgotten and left a pot on and was boiling over. She brought up data sheets on her monitor.

"No," the crewman of the runabout said. "We had the repeater channels open. There was no static."

"Thank you very much. We're sorry for your loss," Thomas said, signing off from the conversation still feeling uneasy. It didn't look like another ship had attacked the runabout. But how could, they be sure?

Martha-Key turned to them, her eyes wide with excitement. "I know where Bohica is."

"Where?" Ned and Thomas asked in unison.

"I realized what happened when you mentioned Frogging Repeaters. I had taken readings on them when we first got here more than two weeks ago. SRL, inter-phase delays, propagation thresholds, LLT, the whole battery of tests."

"What does that have to do with Bohica?"

"Calm down, Thomas, let her finish," said Ivan.

"I ran the tests again last watch but didn't look at the data."

"What did you find?" This time it was Ned's turn to interrupt.

"Something is interfering with the repeaters. They are still working within their parameters, but it's going to get worse. Soon they will be inoperative. Something is in their way ... Bohica."

CHAPTER 16

The Group Master stood up as the envoy entered his room. "I have just received a communication from Fleet Nest," he said, handing a sheet of thick translucent film to the green skin lizard. "They are not happy with the situation. The humans continue to occupy Bohica space."

"That is not my concern," said the Green lizard, "Our leaders have made an agreement and it has been fulfilled. That is all I'm obligated to care about." He looked down to read the translation.

"I'm sure that's comforting to you. I know that reestablishing this region is my responsibility. However, you and I have a new challenge to deal with." The Group Master made sure that the envoy heard the emphasis on the word - YOU.

"They're sending an Overseer?"

"Yes," said the Group Master, "I find them useless and tedious. He will shortly be arriving at the Bohica system."

"I don't see how that makes any difference to what has already happened," the Green lizard said, handing back the film.

"That may be true. But it could change the smell of the future. I think that you would not like or care for that kind of an outcome."

"I agree," the Green lizard said. "Let's hope we can make the future smell better."

* * *

"You've got to be kidding," Ivan said. He was obviously startled by Martha-Keys claim.

"So where is Bohica?" Thomas realized he stared at Martha-Key and felt tension winding up inside him. Finding Bohica has been the most frustrating thing he has ever tried to do.

"Don't you get it?" Ivan said. "The remains of Bohica are in Q-space." He turned to look away. "I never would have guessed that."

"That's right," Martha-Key explained. "The signal of the frogging repeaters on the Q-space side is becoming more degraded. The only explanation is that metal-rich matter is drifting between the signal sources."

"That's why they originally came to Bohica, for the heavy metals." Thomas understood what she said, but how could that be? "Wait a minute. How could they do that? I'm no scientist, but I do know that popping a planet into Q-space would take an enormous amount of energy."

"The gravity spike." Everyone turned and looked at Rusty. Enlightenment again glowed from his face. "If Bohica folded onto itself enough times and the gravity spike was large enough, the matter would collapse to a very small sphere. In doing so, a large amount of energy would be generated."

"The ships," Ned broke in very excited, "that did the time stacking, by being so close, could have absorbed that energy. They could easily open a window to Q-space before they were destroyed. Bohica collapsed and slipped through with the momentum of its normal planetary motion. Then the window would close, time would catch up to the time stacked elements and the remains would expand in Q-space."

"Exactly," Rusty said with a big grin.

"The runabout you talked to," Ivan said.

"Yes," Martha-Key answered, pointing at Ivan. "The runabout hit the debris. And I'll bet that's what made our entry into this system so rough."

Only the hum of the ship drowned out the quiet that remained. The revelations sank in, and their faces turned dark.

"There is only one way to find out," said Taffa-Lee as she moved into the group. "We will need to go far outside what would be Bohica's orbital path."

"Why?" Thomas asked.

"We have no idea of the extent of the debris field."

"What are you talking about?"

"We need to survey this system in Q-space," she said. "If the mass of the debris field is as big as Bohica, then that's where it is." She turned to Rusty. "Warm up the equipment. Ivan, it has been great seeing all of you again. But I think you need to move back to your ship."

"Yes, Ma'am," Ivan said, then turned and made his way to the air lock. "We're coming with you," he yelled over his shoulder, "You'll need an escort."

"Ned, you need to plot a course and get us out of here."

"Wait," said Thomas. "Before we go, I need to talk with Victor and explain what we're doing. He can answer questions that anyone might have and be the official contact."

"Are you sure you want to do that?" Taffa-Lee asked. "Do you trust him that well? Or should we just go do it and tell him later, when we know for sure."

"He deserves to know. I don't think he can get into any trouble. It should be quiet around here," said Thomas.

Martha-Key made the connection and Victor's face appeared on the monitor. "What can I do for you, Thomas?"

"We are going to make another set of long-distance measurements of the system. I would like for you to stay here and be the official presence while we pop out of the system to make them. This could prove, where Bohica is located."

Victor's expression turned serious and apprehensive. "Where is it?"

"We think it's right here, only in Q-space. We also think that's what the runabout ran into before it entered normal-space."

"They've poisoned the system," Victor said, turning his head away from the terminal. The connection abruptly cut off.

Thomas wanted to know what he meant but decided to wait. The *Gold Rat* began to move. He didn't want to tie up any of the resources that might be needed to verify the location of Bohica.

*   *   *

Victor got up from the terminal.

"Are we really going to do that? Stay here and let them go off on their own?" Yen asked, as she turned toward him.

Victor gazed at the blank screen, then abruptly walked to his cabin.

He sat cross-legged on his bunk holding his book to his chest. "So, they found Bohica." He had to say it out loud. The inevitability had never been in question. They were smart and sensible people. But could they figure out who did it? And if they did, would the balance of power stay the same?

He turned the pages in his book until he found what he was looking for. His finger traced Sun Tzu's words.

Now in order to kill the enemy, our men must be roused to anger...

Would that ever happen to the human race? Could they ever again boil with rage against the unjust or had they been beaten down too many times and become content with the subservient life?

It all seemed very comfortable to everyone. Most species were unhappy with their lives, including humans. But the level of discontent remained consistently tolerable. Humanity has been teetering on the edge, but safe. Yes, the universe harbored its share of dangers. Just enough to keep them from boredom. Mediocrity that has gone to seed.

CHAPTER 17

The trip out to where Ned and Taffa-Lee thought it would be safe took forever. So, it seemed to Thomas. Not only that, but the equipment used to take measurements in Q-space was different and difficult to use. It took a while for Rusty to configure everything and have it work right. Finally, it all came together.

"Thomas, you sit here." Rusty indicated a chair next to him at the console. "Since there is no light source in Q-space, we can't see anything. But we can measure the matter, if present."

Everyone gathered around the monitors. Thomas felt his familiar uneasiness creep in. He had been here before and remembered the sting of disappointment.

"The computer will display an artificial view of hyper-space, giving us a context to make sense of the data," Rusty continued.

An image jumped, startling Thomas. He quickly recovered and saw a three-dimensional grid displayed on the screen.

"These contour lines show the gravity well of Bohica's sun."

Thomas began to ask a question, but Rusty beat him to it.

"Before you ask, 'where's Bohica?' it should appear in this area in a few moments." Rusty pointed with his finger. Then a smoky cloud took form on the monitor.

"Look at that," Taffa-Lee said.

"No doubt about it, that's Bohica," Rusty continued. "The detectors haven't been calibrated for Q-space, but the mass is very close to that of Bohica and it can't be anything else."

"Are you sure it's not a natural formation?" Thomas needed to make sure there was no mistake. He had grown tired of disappointment.

"There is no natural matter in Q-space, only what has been put here."

"I think we should analyze a hard sample," Taffa-Lee said, turning to the others. "Ned," she shouted, "move us in closer, but not too fast. We want to get a piece of it."

"On our way," Ned yelled back down from the cockpit.

"The way people move through Q-space," said Rusty, stoking his beard, "it's no wonder they ran into it. No one would ever see it."

"What do you mean?" Thomas asked.

"Navigation in Q-space is done with gravity wells, not mass or light."

"Now I'm confused. I thought mass caused the well."

"The gravity well in Q-space is a reflection of the mass in normal space. It's very different."

"What's the density? And is it changing?" Asked, Taffa-Lee, she had a look that even Thomas worried about.

"It's changing all right," replied Rusty, "The debris field is getting larger and less dense."

"Let's find out how fast it's going and where it's moving to."

"I'm on it," Martha-Key said. "It's going to take a while."

Forcing himself to take it easy, Thomas got up and poured himself a cup of tea. He needed to calm his nerves and the tension that had built up. The entire trip had been an emotional roller-coaster. This was the first time he had seen it coming and had taken steps to smooth it out.

Thomas moved to the table. He sat down and took a deep breath. What else could he do. Angelica was dead. Bohica had been destroyed. Everyone on that planet was gone. They didn't know who did it or why. And to top everything else, there was nothing he or any other humans could do about it.

*　　*　　*

Victor looked up from his book. Yen stood in the doorway of his cabin.

"A Surrien ship is moving to dock with us. They insist on talking to the human representative. I wasn't sure how serious you were about keeping up this false identity."

"I don't want to talk to the Surriens. Tell them to go away."

"I've tried that. A bishop from their religious cast is very angry and demands to talk with you in person. He says he will use force if necessary."

Victor wondered if Thomas had these kinds of irritating problems to put up with. If so, Victor may have to up Thomas's status in his mind. At first, he didn't want to deal with them, but thought better of it. "You tell his eminence that he may dock. I will join him on his ship in one hour. We'll let him stew awhile."

If love was the essence of the religions of man, then time was the spiritual nature of the Surriens. Their bishop would be interesting. This could be an opportunity to find out what they know. He could filter the information later for Thomas.

Victor leisurely read more in his book. He came upon a passage that had always struck him. So obvious and truthful, yet so misunderstood.

All warfare is based on deception.

When he had finished his reading, he freshened up before meeting with the Surriens.

After stepping on board, the Bishop's ship, Victor could tell how irritated his holiness had become. The Surriens were tall thin mammal-like creatures who walked upright and were covered with fine gray fur. Usually, this quiet and polite species would have welcomed Victor aboard. Instead, he confronted a raving animal, who's brightly colored tunic fluttered about everywhere.

Victor's translator on his belt spat and sputtered out incomprehensible gibberish. The Holy-man's two attendants, dressed in the more traditional bib, boots and knee pads, said nothing.

"Excuse me, your Holiness," Victor said just below a scream. "I humbly apologize," he continued in a normal tone, "for keeping you this long. But I had urgent business that couldn't wait."

"This is intolerable." The translator could finally make out the Bishops words. "Wasting the time of the emissary of the Surrien Church is an insult."

"Forgive me for the delay." Victor lowered his head and did a half bow. He chose his words carefully. "Your patience has afforded us the interval to save several lives. And for that, we are unendingly grateful."

During the long silence the Bishop relaxed, but the expression on his thin lips and large brown eyes remained intent. "The Enduring Continuum Clergy of the Surrien Realm are ever vigilant for the hardships of others. We hope your efforts will continue to be fruitful."

"The churches of Humanity thank you. What brings your Eminence to this humble servant of my people?"

"The monks at the Flowing Waters Monastery on Hector detected a quiver in TIME. With devoted meditation on their sacred instruments, the location of the disturbance pointed here. At a system where a human colony has conveniently disappeared."

"I'm not sure what you are implying." Victor told the truth. All the visitors to this system knew that Bohica was gone. The Humans weren't keeping the disappearance a secret.

"We are a calm race and do not impose the religious realities of the universe onto others. Most species believe in some form of TIME. But this blasphemy cannot be allowed to go unpunished. The manipulation of temporal stability is not for us mortals. Only Divine intervention can truly deviate TIME. All else is the scant shadow of heresy. Humans must suffer for this abomination."

Victor had not considered the possibility of the holy-man's reaction. It all made sense, considering their religious bent. It was interesting that they could tell what had happened and where. That was information he would investigate later.

"What makes you think that the Humans are responsible for this obvious transgression?" Victor asked.

"You were using the planet. It was isolated, lonely, an out of the way place. It would be perfect for such a diabolical experiment. What else could it be?"

"All that is incorrect. In fact, we are the victims here. We have no idea who could have done this horrendous act. We were given no warning. And as far as we know, thousands of humans have lost their lives. Murdered by the same heretics you seek." Victor felt good about putting this Bishop in his place.

"Is that true?"

"Yes, of course, and I can prove it to you. But we have heard of your monks at the monastery. Victor lied. With your knowledge and sacred instruments, you have become the more likely suspect. We believe that perhaps you did this terrible thing. And if we find out that you have . . ."

"I give you my assurance that no Surrien has taken part in performing this black art." The Bishop's expression had changed. His eyes had sincerity and were apologetic. He stepped forward and put long, slender fingers on Victor's shoulder. "If your evidence can show that Humans were not involved and did not corrupt time, then I promise to do whatever I can to help you find who did."

"I am so glad to hear that." Victor tried not to smile. "If you would join me on my ship, I have some interesting data to show you. It was taken from a survey ship we hired to investigate this tragedy."

"I would be honored, if you would share that with me."

Back on board his ship, Victor showed the Surrien Bishop the data that the *Gold Rat* had taken. The displays of the ships diving toward Bohica, the high-speed data, the theory about time stacking one planet on top of another and allowing it to explode into Q-space. It was compelling evidence and the Bishop agreed.

"Thank you. I will take this data back to the monastery for prayer and analysis," said the Bishop, his sincerity ringing true. "Be assured, when the blasphemers have been found, the Surriens will stand with Humanity."

Victor's emotions were not always visible but this time he couldn't hide them. "Thank you, from all Humanity."

CHAPTER 18

"I think we're close enough," Taffa-Lee shouted to Ned, "we can drift into it from here."

Thomas watched over her shoulder as she manipulated the screen. He could hear and feel the change in the *Gold Rat* as it came to a stop. He didn't understand exactly what Taffa-Lee was doing. He only knew she was trying to retrieve a sample of the dust cloud that had once been Bohica.

"There, we have it. This will take a few minutes," she said, turning to Thomas. "I have to prepare the sample and then run it through the GCR for analysis. Relax for a while."

"Thomas," Martha-Key added, "you've been under a lot of strain. You need to take some time."

As Taffa-Lee went aft, Thomas poured another cup of tea and sat down next to Lee-Hope. She had started her homework.

"What are you studying now?"

"History."

"That's a big subject. What part?"

"The Bernardo Migration."

"I always thought that was interesting. It was such an optimistic time that turned out so wrong. We were so naive about the dangers out in the universe."

"Is there going to be a war?" She looked at him with all the innocence he had ever imagined a young girl could have. Did she know about war? Maybe she had read about it or had seen the dramas.

"I don't think so, only if the people who did this terrible thing to Bohica are small and weak. Humans don't have the capability to put together a force to strike back. And if it was the Tri-Bah, it wouldn't be smart to start a fight with them."

"But I thought you were angry."

"Yes, I'm very upset."

"It seems to me," she said, "that history is full of wars that were started for sillier reasons than this."

Thomas didn't know how to answer. He had always felt that war should never be a reaction. The act of starting a war seemed ignorant and uncivilized. He also felt that calculating and planning a war was cold and just plain wrong. The only true winners were the ones who solved a problem without a fight. "War is a no-win situation. Everyone loses."

Lee-Hope went back to her reading and Thomas finished his tea.

Taffa-Lee came up to Thomas and handed him one of several clear tubes half full of coarse-grained material. It looked like ground volcanic rock.

"Is this it?" Thomas searched her face for signs of an explanation.

"Yes, that's Bohica." Other members of the *Gold Rat* gathered around to look at the samples. "It appears to be a cooled, plasma treated silicone with the same percentage of minerals as Bohica."

"That's in keeping with our theory on the time stacking," Martha-Key added.

"I also found small traces of carbon," Taffa-Lee said softly.

Thomas didn't need an explanation to know what that meant. Bohica was a lifeless rock. The carbon could have been part of someone on Bohica when it was destroyed. Maybe a few atoms of Angelica were in the tube.

"I thought you might want to keep that one."

"Thank you." Thomas looked down at the small tube in his hand. What would he tell his wife? How could he give her only this to make up for her loss? He put the small tube into a safe pocket of his jump suit.

"I have those numbers for the expansion of the cloud," Martha-Key said, turning to the terminal. She pointed out some figures to Taffa-Lee but talked to everyone. "In another month, this system will be unapproachable."

"What do you mean?" Thomas asked.

"You will have to pop into normal space far away from the system to keep from hitting the cloud. It will be uneconomical to even come here. It will stay like that for more than thirty years. Then the cloud will have dissipated enough to permit ships to pass through the region. Even then it will be difficult."

"They poisoned the system." Everyone looked at Thomas. "That's what Victor told me."

"He's right," Rusty said. "Is it possible for this cloud to drift into the Neca system? It's the closest to Bohica."

"It will be safe by the time it gets that far."

Thomas held up the vial. "How can some grains of sand be that dangerous?"

"At the speeds we travel, it's like hitting solid rock. That grit can chew up the hull of a ship in seconds."

"So, this is what happened to that damaged runabout." Thomas began to understand the extent to which Bohica's destruction was affecting this system. It seemed more than a hostile act. Could someone want this region to be inaccessible? "You realize that this makes the question of 'why' that much bigger."

"We know, Thomas."

To put the entire system out of touch for that long required very long-term thinking. Bohica was already a remote place. If the aggression were meant just for the humans, conventional weapons would have worked and been much cheaper. Who would gain from such an act?

"We're not alone," Martha-Key said, frantically adjusting the monitor.

"Who is it?" Asked Thomas.

"We have watched ships enter the system as long as we have been out here. But they have been one or two at a time. We now have sixteen ships on a polar approach. Some are big," Martha-Key said. "See that one is very large, six good size and nine smaller."

"One Stone class, three Bolder class, three support and nine Rock class ships. What are they doing here?" Said Taffa-Lee

"It's a Tri-Bah Subgroup," Rusty said to Thomas.

"I know. Maybe we should get back to normal space."

*   *   *

"We have entered normal space inside the Bohica system," the Subgroup Commander reported.

The Group Master never tired of this moment. The excitement gnawing at the gizzard heightened the sensations soldiers felt at approaching confrontation. This was what he trained to do, and he loved it.

"Launch the Pebble Fighters. Set up and patrol a perimeter. I want them at a safe distance," he said, pointing to signals on a display. "Have a Rock ship assess the threat from the ships in the area."

"Yes, Group Master. Shall we monitor their communications and gather electronic intelligence as well?"

"Whatever you think would be necessary. Just don't make it a top priority. If any inquiries are made, tell them I will make an all-ships announcement soon."

"Yes, Group Master."

"I'll be in my quarters if you have information." He turned and walked out of the room. His mind uneasy over the number of ships in the system. He hadn't expected so many, not that he was worried. If they wanted to fight, it would have happened by now. He didn't believe they would start any trouble. There was nothing to gain, and it would be unwise on their part. But they could be stubborn about leaving.

He rested in his cabin until he heard the signal from his Sub Group Commander. "Enter," he said.

"We have the threat assessment, Group Master."

"Tell me."

"A total of ninety-two ships was found in the system. Eighteen have left, all non-humans. Of the remaining seventy-four, most are human with the next largest group being Surrien."

The Group Master thought it was unusual for the Surriens to pay this much attention to other people's business.

"Five large escorts and eight smaller escorts seem to make up the majority of the threats," the Commander continued. "There are an additional twenty-one ships that have minor defensive capabilities."

The Group Master stepped closer and gave his Commander a hard look. "What is your analysis?"

"I estimate 20 percent."

"Good." He could easily deal with that. A 100 percent would be a force equal to them. "One-fifth of our firepower and they're amateurs at best. Move us into a frontal defensive posture and signal me when we're in position. I will be in communications. That's all."

He made his way through the dimly lit corridors to the com center. The room was filled with rows of consoles, each attended by a busy Tri-Bah. The Group Master liked to visit this room. He always marveled at the energy and activity that took place. Personnel were communicating and exchanging data with ships in the group, some with other groups and some with other parts of the ship. The officer in charge approached and waited for orders.

"I need to make an all-ships broadcast to everyone in this system. I don't want it going through Q-space, just a local transmission."

"It will take a few moments to set up."

"Take what time you need. I will give the message from the bridge."

"Yes, Group Master."

Leaving the com center, the Group Master visualized what he would say. He needed to clear this system and get everybody on their way back to normal. He would use simple, firm and direct words. They must leave. Nothing was left here for them, nothing.

CHAPTER 19

"I would like to talk with Victor," Thomas said, right after they popped back into normal space.

Martha-Key went to work on the console. She turned to Thomas and motioned him to the screen. Victor's aged face appeared in the monitor.

"Thomas, I'm glad you're back." An amusing smile came through his gray beard. "I had the most interesting conversation with a Surrien Bishop. You will never guess what they think is going on."

"Maybe later, Victor. The Tri-Bah are coming. A Subgroup should be popping in at any moment. We watched them approach. We also found Bohica. Or should I say, what's left of it."

Victor's face turned joyless. "You didn't really expect to find it intact."

"I couldn't let go of that hope until I saw it for myself."

"Of course, however, we need to move on."

"You're right, of course. Would you like to be here when we talk with them? I could use your advice. You may have some good questions to ask."

"Of course, Thomas, I'll be right there."

Soon after Victor stepped aboard the *Gold Rat* and was greeted by Thomas, the intercom sounded that the Tri-Bah Subgroup had appeared. Thomas could feel the tension rise.

"They don't seem to be in a hurry," Taffa-Lee said.

"That's good," Rusty said. "If they wanted to start something, they would have come in a lot hotter than that. They'd have been all over us by now."

"Thomas, you don't mind if we have Ivan Black listening in when we talk with the Tri-Bah?" Taffa-Lee asked.

For the first time he saw a soft pleading on her face. He had seen that look in his wife, when she asked him to be careful and find out what happened to Angelica-So. There had been other occasions. It always touched him softly.

"I suppose it would make things much easier if we do it now, instead of relaying it later?" Said Thomas, giving in to the request.

"Yes, it would," she said with a smile.

"Sure. In fact, I would be interested in knowing what he thinks."

"Thank you, Thomas."

"All right," Thomas said, raising his voice so everyone could hear. "Let's talk with them and find out what this is all about."

"Whenever you're ready," Martha-Key said.

He took a deep breath before starting. "Good traveling, Subgroup Commander. I'm Thomas McCormick and with me is Victor Wiseman. We are Representatives of the Union of Humanity. We would like to discuss the situation that has happened here at Bohica." A short silence followed.

"The Group Master will issue an all-ships communication shortly. Please stand by," said a voice from the Tri-Bah.

Quiet.

"That wasn't very friendly," Victor said. "Maybe you should try again."

"I'm sorry if there is some misunderstanding." Thomas fought to keep his voice under control. "We are official Representatives of the Union of Humanity. We can speak for every human here and act for the Union. We . . ."

"There is no misunderstanding. The Group Master will issue an all-ships communication shortly. Please stand by."

"They're treating us like children," Ivan Black's voice came through the monitor.

"They certainly are," Martha-Key said softly.

"Let's see what they have to say, and then try again afterwards," Thomas said, fighting to keep his anger from showing. He felt he hadn't succeeded and was tired of caring if it showed or not.

"They're changing the deployment of the Subgroup," Victor said. "It looks like a frontal formation."

"That would be very naive," Ivan added.

"I was thinking the same thing. It's probably more posturing than anything else," said Victor.

"Why is that naive?" Thomas asked.

"The Tri-Bah are used to taking on larger ships, like the ones they have. But a small ship could speed toward them, pop into Q-space, pass them, pop back into normal space, turn one eighty and, as we use to say, shoot them in the ass."

"That doesn't seem very fair."

"Remember, Thomas, all warfare is based on deception. Fair has nothing to do with it," said Victor with a grin.

Thomas could see in Victor's eyes that he knew what he was talking about. He had a passion for its truth that Thomas could understand. For the first time he wondered who Victor really was and what he was doing here. Neither one of them was acting like a bureaucrat.

"I think it's time for the announcement," Martha-Key said.

"This is Ta-hesss, Group Master of the Stone Wall Battle-Group and the Second Arm of the Turret War-Group. This is a command statement from the Tri-Bah Nest. You are to dissipate immediately. This is Tri-Bah controlled space and there is no longer any reason for any ship to be in this system."

Silence.

"That's about what I expected," Ivan said.

"Me to, but it's unacceptable." Thomas put his head in his hands and tried to think about what he should do next. He could make his report to Rodriguez and go home. That had a nice sense of finality. Still, doesn't seem right. He could yell and scream at the Tri-Bah. He imagined himself in a tiny ship brandishing his fist at the large Tri-Bah fleet as they left him alone in the empty system.

Thomas took a deep breath to steady his nerves and muster all the authority he could. "We have a treaty to this space for mining. It was made with the Tri-Bah Nest. We have every right to be here."

"What are you mining?" Came the reply.

"We were mining the small planet, Bohica."

"We can't identify the planet Bohica. It is not here. You are to leave immediately."

Silence.

"Thomas," said Martha-Key.

"What."

"We're getting a lot of chatter from the others. And many of them want to know what you're going to do." Martha-Key's voice held a bit of surprise.

Thomas lifted his head. "What are they saying?"

"They don't want to leave until they know what happened to the people here. Some of them had family on Bohica. Others are just outraged."

Thomas turned to Victor. "What do you think we should do?"

"That's not up to me. This is your operation. But I would like to ask, what do you want to do?"

"Get to the truth of what happened here." It seemed so simple in Thomas' mind.

"Well then, do it," Victor said.

Thomas, somehow, felt lifted. He had been too concerned about Rodriguez and doing his job correctly. The strain of all this intrigue had dulled his senses. Victor successfully cut through the clutter and gave Thomas permission to do what was right. "Can we do an all-ships transmission?"

"Certainly," Martha-Key said, as she worked the terminal. "Go ahead."

"This is Thomas McCormick, Representative of the Union of Humanity. I urge everyone to stay. The Tri-Bah Nest owes us an explanation as to what happened here. I can say for certain that Bohica has been destroyed and thousands of humans have lost their lives due to some apparent treachery. We demand information from the Tri-Bah Group Master."

Thomas sat back in the chair. He wondered if anyone would be convinced to stay and pressure the Tri-Bah to talk. Most people had better things to do than to push a giant rock up a hill, just to see it roll back down.

"There is a lot of conversation, most of it for staying. Some are sending their own message to the Tri-Bah, urging them to talk with us. Would you like to listen in?" Martha-Key adjusted the terminal so Thomas could hear.

Thomas felt good inside by the voices of so many insignificant people demanding a statement from the mighty fire-lizards. He doubted if it would do any good. The Tri-Bah were hard to push around.

"They're doing another all-ships transmission," said Martha-Key.

"This is a command statement from the Tri-Bah Nest. You are to dissipate immediately. This is Tri-Bah controlled space and there is no longer any reason for any ship to be in this system."

"I want to answer that," said Thomas

She keyed the terminal and nodded in his direction.

"This is Thomas McCormick, of the Union of Humanity. We have every reason to be here. Our people have died, and we deserve an explanation. These people had a contract with you in your controlled space. That makes the Tri-Bah responsible. We demand to speak with you in person about this matter."

*　*　*

The Group Master could not understand these animals. Why wouldn't they leave? He didn't want to force the issue. Military action was a poor substitute for diplomacy. You can build an empire with force, but you sustain it with diplomacy.

He pushed the switch to transmit. "Meeting and talking accomplishes nothing. It would be better for everyone to go back to their commercial enterprises. There is nothing left here."

The reply was quick.

"All we want is to express our concerns and discuss the situation."

Humming of his ship and dim lighting added to the feeling that this small system was closing in. The Group Master heard the determination in the message, but also heard an opportunity.

"Representatives of Humanity, I grant you a short meeting on my ship, the Inner Stone. My Sub Group Commander will work with you to make the preparations. One last thought before we meet - - my patience is dwindling."

The Group Master needed to make this into a victory. He turned to his second-in-command. "If all they want is to express their concerns, then we can afford to listen. Set up a meeting place and arrange for armed guards. Find out if the humans need any special requirements and make them feel comfortable."

"Yes, Group Master, who will be attending?"

"We will let them have three. We will have The Overseer and the Green lizard, along with myself. That will make it even. That is, except for the armed guards. Arrange it quickly. I want to finish this quickly."

CHAPTER 20

"So, who are we going to get for the third person?" Thomas asked, sitting across from Victor drinking his tea.

"What about the second?"

"I thought you and I would go, and we would need someone else as a third."

"You should be there, but not me," Victor said. "Like I mentioned, this is your meeting. Someone has to stay here and watch with a cool eye and feed you information if necessary."

"Maybe you're right. Do you have any ideas?"

"I've got one," Taffa-Lee said, as she sat down next to Thomas. "Ivan Black or one of his people would be a great asset. They know the space around here and should have some great insights."

"That sounds good," Victor said.

"I have a suggestion for the other." Came a voice from behind them.

They turned around to Martha-Key at the communications console. She had been listening to the messages between the human ships.

"Who would that be?" Thomas asked.

"A freighter captain named Zavala. He has been vocal about the situation making some good arguments and yet keeps calm. He would do well representing the rest of the ships."

"Invite them onboard," Thomas said.

It wasn't long before they met Ivan Black's cousin, Philip Black. He had spent most of his life in or near Tri-Bah space. He turned out to be the closest thing to an expert they had.

"You may already know by size and numbers that we are dealing with a Tri-Bah Subgroup," Philip Black said. "There are two other

Subgroups somewhere else making their presence known. These are all under the Group Master. The Sub Group Commander here is the most junior of the three. This way the Group Master can train and guide his Sub Group Commanders."

"Most of us know that much," Thomas said. "Can you tell us anything about the one we're dealing with?"

"This Tri-Bah Group has patrolled this region for a few years. The Group Master, Ta-hesss, is generally honest and fair. He will usually leave you alone unless you cause a problem. They are quick to stop any disturbance. And I'm sure he sees this gathering of ships as a disruption to the trade routes. His officers are concise and have little tolerance for foolishness."

"We'll keep that in mind," Thomas said.

A new person stepped into the crowded room. "Namaste, everyone, I'm Captain Zavala."

"Welcome to the *Gold Rat*," Ned said.

After the introductions, Thomas had a concern about Zavala. He seemed too eager to make light of the conversations with the others. They needed someone serious.

"Captain Zavala, you have been nominated to be on this delegation. Please tell me why you think you can contribute," Thomas asked, trying not to offend his good nature.

"I've been pushing freight out here to Bohica since the beginning. I've seen the operation grow and develop over the months. I enjoyed coming here. They shared their food and hospitality with me and my crew. They were friends. And I think whoever did this, should pay."

"Negotiating with non-humans," Ivan said, "can be stressful and irritating. We all need to be on our toes and keep our wits handy. Do you think you can handle that, Captain Zavala?"

"Yes, I have worked with creatures like these before."

"You sound qualified to me," Thomas said. Everyone agreed.

"One more thing," Taffa-Lee interjected. "They've agreed to the double-loop broadcast of the meeting. This means that we will see it all and will know if anyone has tampered with the feed. Good luck. We will be docking with the *Inner Stone* shortly."

Thomas could feel the excitement and hear it in the voices. It hadn't been like this since Black first arrived. He didn't want to get his hopes up. It had been a long search for the answers. The fire lizards might not have the patience for him to learn any more.

"Mr. McCormick."

Thomas turned and found Lee-Hope looking up at him. "What can I do for you?"

"I just wanted to say what an honor it has been serving you, and hope you had a pleasant stay aboard the *Gold Rat*. Please travel with us again."

"Even though you are supposed to say that I'll just be gone for a while. I still have a claim on my bunk." This brought a smile to her face.

"Of Course, you'll be right back. I'm just practicing."

A gentle nudge to the ship signaled that they had docked with the *Inner Stone*.

Thomas pointed his finger at Lee-Hope. "Don't forget your schoolwork."

"I won't."

Taffa-Lee put her hand on Thomas' shoulder, "Remember they're not going to let us stay docked. So be sure to have them send us a message when you want to be picked up."

"Don't worry, I'm not likely to stick around any longer than I have to."

Thomas moved to the airlock with the others. The most notable change Thomas encountered when he stepped aboard the *Inner Stone* was an assaulting antiseptic smell. The biting odor might have been normal for a fire lizard ship, but Thomas wondered if they disinfected the ship to prevent the spread of human cooties.

The pressure and temperature seemed pleasant enough. A short way down the corridor from the airlock a Tri-Bah officer put up his paws, palm out, and stopped their advance.

"You agreed to bring no weapons," he said.

"That's right, and we didn't bring any," Thomas replied.

"What about that?" The fire lizard pointed to the Kanashimi knife strapped to Thomas' right thigh.

"That may technically be a weapon, but it's traditional. It's meant for defense." Thomas knew the others felt the same about giving up their knifes. Without it, some humans felt desperately naked.

"The Group Master says you must remove them. If you do not, there will be no talk."

Philip stepped forward and stood next to Thomas. "Tell your Group Master that we will remove our knives if you remove your teeth and claws."

*   *   *

The Tri-Bah Group Master watched on a monitor from a communications alcove near the meeting room as the humans were confronted. It was a good observation by his security officer to stop them. The human obsession with their knives seemed ridiculous. It wasn't a practical weapon, and they shouldn't have brought them.

"You're not going to allow them to bring weapons aboard your ship, are you? That would be seven kinds of foolish."

The Group Master knew the slippery voice of the green envoy. Why did it irritate him so? It wasn't clear why a visitor should be telling him what the protocols should be within his command, on his ship.

"I thought you were told to remain in the waiting room."

"You mustn't allow these ignorant animals any concession. They haven't earned the right to anything. After all, the demonstration proved successful. There is no need to even talk with these creatures."

"Quiet."

The Green lizard's eyelids opened wide as he stared back at the Group Master.

"Do not forget your place as a guest." The Group Master keyed the communications device. "Let them enter and they may keep their knives." He said this to upset the envoy. The humans would be more attentive if they didn't have their knives. That would be a small concession to pay. "Now, get back to the waiting room."

*   *   *

The sentry led the three humans down passageways and into a large room with plenty of space around a long brown table made of a fibrous plant material. Its smooth polished finish and rich dark hue contrasted against the cold metal surfaces of the walls and floor.

Thomas speculated that this was an obvious extravagance to use such a material on a military ship. No chairs, floor covering, or pictures hung on the walls. The table dominated the sparse surroundings.

Six Tri-Bah stood guard. One on either side of the door and four others ringed the room. They were carrying small weapons on their belts.

The three humans moved to one side of the table. Thomas found himself on the end, waiting for something to happen. This was as close as he had come to the answer. He knew the how, what, when and where, but two things were left to discover, the who and the why.

"I guess we're going to stand," Zavala said.

"Isn't that normal, Philip?" Thomas asked.

"Yes, either standing or lying on the floor. In this case, I think I would prefer to be on my feet."

A Tri-Bah of some importance walked into the room. Behind him came the Green lizard that Thomas had seen only once before. The tunic was the same, as well as the pattern of the gold snowflake on his left paw.

"What is that?" Philip whispered, leaning toward Thomas.

"I'm sure that was the one at the bar on Fallen giving me all kind of cryptic messages." Thomas wondered if the fire lizards and this new player were working together? What could that mean for the humans and the other species in this region of space?

As he pondered the future of humanity, Thomas realized a large spike lizard with his glowing red eyes had joined them at the table. Thomas recognized one of its six horns. The left rear horn tip was broken.

"Tee, is that you?"

"Namaste, Thomas, are you well?"

Chapter 21

"That has to be the Green lizard Thomas met on Fallen," Taffa-Lee said, watching the monitors showing the meeting room. "See the gold tattoo on his left hand."

"Yes, but is it the same one or is it his boss?" Victor asked. "They could all have that mark."

"We'll have to ask Thomas later."

"Look at the spike lizard. Those are rare," Rusty said.

"I'm fine, Tee," Thomas said through the translator. "What are you doing here?"

"I'm sorry, Thomas, I have been ordered too only observe this meeting and not interfere or answer any questions."

As introductions were being made in the meeting room, Victor remembered his talk with Armondo on Mitzul. Thomas' friend told him that a spike lizard had visited Thomas before he left. He hadn't thought much of it then. Thomas had many acquaintances through his work of negotiating contracts. Yet it seemed surprising that one of the gray monsters would show up here. And yet, they had always been a mystery.

Victor's attention was drawn back to the images in front of him. The new lizard had been introduced as an envoy from friends of the Tri-Bah.

"Isn't it interesting?" Victor said. "The Fire lizards have many friends, yet I don't see them at the table. Just the one we've never seen before."

"That means he is important to Bohica," Lee-Hope said, looking at Victor.

Victor couldn't hold back a smile. "Yes."

The introductions were over, and the Group Master gestured across the table. "McCormick, you had something to say."

"Yes. We would like to know what happened to Bohica," Thomas said, wondering how many times he had asked that question.

"Why are you talking to the Tri-Bah," asked the Group Master?

"The agreement between us, Correspondence Pact number zero five five five dash four two, states that humans are permitted to establish a settlement on Bohica, residing in Tri-Bah controlled space. The purpose is to develop the mineral potential of that planet. In return, 28 percent of all the ore exported is to go to the Tri-Bah. In addition . . ."

"I'm aware of the agreement we made with the humans."

"Then why have you shucked your responsibility?"

"What is that?"

"To maintain the security and safety of Bohica and its population." Thomas did his best to keep his voice at an even tone.

"That was a human responsibility."

"Where does it say that in the agreement?"

"It is implied."

"How?"

"People should take care of their own. There was no Tri-Bah on Bohica, and therefore we do not care what happens."

That was an unusually cold statement, even from a fire lizard. They were being standoffish and vague, and the lack of cooperation made Thomas uneasy. He wondered if they had something to do with it. This did not ease his frustration, only heightened it.

"And what about the people on Bohica?" Philip asked.

"They were your responsibility," the Group Master said.

"We disagree," Thomas interjected. "If it was Tri-Bah controlled space, then it was the Tri-Bah's responsibility to protect Bohica and the humans on it," he said, his voice rising.

"No. Humans are responsible for humans wherever they are in space."

Thomas shook his head, how absurd. There had never been a precedent for this attitude from the Tri-Bah.

Captain Zabala leaned over to Thomas and whispered, "He has a talent of not answering your original question."

"You're right." Thomas felt foolish. He had allowed the discussion to drift far from where he started. "Let us leave the responsibility issue behind. I would like to go back to the beginning. What happened to Bohica?"

"Hissst." The Green lizard's words wouldn't translate.

The Group Master shot him a look, then returned his attention to the table. "Bohica no longer belongs to the realm of Tri-Bah space. It is in Q-space. We took data on it as we approached. We are willing to share that information with you." "That won't be necessary," Thomas' voice cracked. "We know where it is. We need to know who did it and why?" He realized his muscles in his arms and chest were tight. He had gotten too close and emotional about Bohica.

"It is no longer useful to you, or the Tri-Bah. The Correspondence Pact no longer applies. I suggest you go home."

"That's unacceptable," Philip said.

"Accept it or not. That's the way it is," said the Group Master strongly.

Before Thomas could answer that cold blooded statement, the spike lizard stepped toward the Group Master and talked quietly with him.

The fire lizard looked to the others at the table. "Excuse us for a moment?" Then the two of them walked out of the room.

Captain Zavala and Philip moved toward the wall and began to whisper. Thomas took a deep breath and tried to relax.

"Why are you still here?" The question from the Green lizard set Thomas back on edge.

Thomas hadn't cared for their conversation on Fallen. And now they were at it again. They both started to walk slowly toward the end of the table. "Where should I be if not here?"

"You should go back and do what you were doing before you came here."

Why were they treating humans like small children that had wandered into vehicle traffic? A cold shiver ran up Thomas' back. Did they really think humans were infantile?

"The real question," Thomas asked, "may not be why am I still here, but why are you here at all?"

"That was explained," said the Green lizard.

"No, it wasn't." Thomas felt a resurgence of determination.

"We are friends of the Tri-Bah."

"That doesn't explain who you are, where your kind comes from, your intentions, and in general the nature of your presence in relation to us," Thomas said, staring into its large yellow eyes.

"All of that is unnecessary at this time."

"We don't think so."

"We don't care. Hisssst."

Thomas found himself standing in front of the green envoy. He never had the feeling of revulsion toward lizards like many humans did. But this one gave Thomas a don't-turn-your-back kind of fear. "Did you destroy Bohica?"

"It is gone, go home."

"Was it you and the Tri-Bah, or just you?" Indignation and rage overwhelmed Thomas.

"Why do you insist on lingering here?"

"Did you kill those people on Bohica?"

"Mourn if you must but go home."

"I had family on that settlement. I knew those people. How dare you talk to me about mourning?" Thomas felt his anger rise.

"They are gone. Go!" The words from the lizard were short and quick.

"Did you kill them?"

The yellow eyes turned from him as to walk away, then snapped back.

"Did you do this?" Thomas shouted!

"Go away."

"No!" Thomas slammed his fist onto the table. "Did you destroy Bohica?"

"Yes," the Green lizard snarled, slapping his left paw onto the table. "We crushed them like bugs." The teeth of the envoy leered out at Thomas' face.

Thomas' hand undid the snap and slid his knife from the sheath in one smooth motion, as he had practiced so many times. With all his anger, he drove the point through the arrogant gold snowflake tattoo on the back of the green marbled paw and as deep into the fibrous table as he could. His knife was sharp. "You bastard." Thomas stood in shock of his actions.

"Aaaaa Ggggg." The envoy's free paw caught Thomas in the head, and he flew backwards, slamming against the floor.

Two guards grabbed Thomas and lifted him to his feet. They pinned him against the wall, one on each side. Thomas tried to kick and move his arms but couldn't.

"My kill," shouted the green lizard.

Captain Zabala and Philip Black drew their blades and rushed to help Thomas. They never got there. The sentries at the door shot them with energy weapons.

The lizard roared as he pulled the knife from the table and his green flesh and tossed it aside. He took slow steps to stand in front of Thomas and extended one long claw.

Unable to break free from the sinewy grip of the Tri-Bah guards, Thomas only wished he could have seen Elizabeth-Charm. At least one more time to tell her the fate of her sister and to smell her hair.

The green envoy thrust his claw deep into Thomas' side. Pain shot through his body. As the claw twisted and rotated in the wound, Thomas fell limp.

Chapter 22

The spike lizard loomed, head and horns above the Group Master. "How long will this deception go on?"

"It will be many years, with any luck." The Group Master walked them down a corridor out of range of the other translators, where no one could overhear. "Our mission now is to get this sector back to normal. We won't try to convince the humans of anything but to get on with their dreary lives."

"They seem more stubborn than usual," Tee said.

"Yes. They have insisted on expressing their concerns. I'm letting them do that. This will not take long. All we must do is let them talk and not answer any questions. They will exhaust their anger and learn nothing. Then we can force them to leave."

A Tri-Bah officer ran to the Group Master. "Forgive me for interrupting, but you must return, immediately." The sound of weapons fire could be heard from the meeting room."

*   *   *

Thomas' action surprised even Victor. Thomas didn't seem like a violent person.

"Taffa-Lee," Ned shouted.

She dropped the pot of tea she was making and rushed back to the monitor. She froze with the others as they watched the green beast knocking Thomas across the room and pulling Thomas' knife from his paw. They clearly heard the claim, "My kill." Someone gasped as Philip Black and Captain Zavala were shot and fell to the floor. And again, when the lizard stabbed Thomas in the side with his claw.

Thomas slumped forward then collapsed. When the other two lizards ran into the room, the Group Master shouted orders.

The whole scene felt unreal, like a theatrical performance. Everyone's attention was transfixed by the image on the screen. Then it all disappeared. The Tri-Bah stopped transmitting.

Lee-Hope dashed over and buried her head in her mother's arms. Taffa-Lee hugged her as only a mother could. She obviously needed the embrace as much as her child did. Taking her daughter's hand, she led them to the Gold Rat living quarters.

These are hard lessons she must learn, Victor thought. Life is an endangered state.

"Lousy lizards," Rusty said.

"Ivan?" Martha-Key said, trying to reestablish contact with the *Black Watch*. She wiped away a tear.

"Yes," he snapped. His anger projected well.

"We are so sorry about Philip."

"Thank you," Ivan answered dryly. "I suggest you move into Q-space and make your way to your next destination."

"Why?" Ned asked.

"Some are leaving. But this treachery cannot go unanswered. Many are moving into positions to fight. It's going to get chaotic around here. You're not a combat ship like we are. You need to get the *Gold Rat* far away."

"You can't be serious," insisted Ned. "Look, Ivan, even with all of the ships hear, taking on a Sub Group is not smart. The other two Sub Groups could be nearby."

"I'm sorry, Ned, but they crossed a line. I would have done the same as Thomas. Even more!"

"Ivan, they've got transponder ID on all of us. If they wanted to, they could hunt us all down."

"Maybe, but this has gone way too far." The tension in Ivan's voice grew thick. "They murdered people. Members of our family. Those snake-tongues are not getting away with it."

Victor hadn't heard that name in a long time. The old insult conjured up all kinds of evil.

Rusty intently watched a monitor. "It's started. Several ships have fired on the Tri-Bah."

"Get out of here, Ned." Ivan's voice was stern. "I've got to go."

"Wait a minute, Ivan." Victor quickly moved to the terminal. "The Tri-Bah fleet is far enough outside the Bohica debris field to safely use Q-space. The larger Stone and Rock class ships are vulnerable from behind. The best tactic is to pop into Q-space, move to change your vector, then jump back to normal space, shoot and then jump again. Also, switch off your translator when communicating. That will at least make things harder on them."

"Thanks, Victor, but we already knew that. I'm afraid most of the other ships are not that sophisticated with combat tactics. You should be advising them."

"I will." Victor was surprised he had agreed but didn't regret it.

"With a strategy like that you'll need their exact locations." Ned's voice sounded hesitant. "We have the detectors to do that from a distance."

"That would be a great advantage," Victor interrupted him.

"I agree," Ivan said, "but Ned, be careful."

"We will, right after we make a delivery. Rusty, reconfigure the detectors to track the Tri-Bah ships and set all the other port buffers for communications."

"I'm halfway there."

Ned grabbed Victor's hand and shook it. "Sorry to kick you out, but we have to move."

"We'll keep in touch." Victor was already moving to the airlock. "Send me the data on ship positions and help me communicate with other ships."

"We will. Now get out of here." Ned's voice was impatient.

Victor scrambled through the small portal between the two ships. His vessel was no more than a runabout. He couldn't fight alongside them directly, but he could help guide them.

He hit the controls for the air lock and stepped into the *Tank Man*. It finally was time to act. This was not what he wanted. He liked being a spy, out of sight. Yoshio should be here. This was his expertise.

"Is McCormick dead?" One of the two women watching a monitor asked.

"Most likely."

"And some of the ships are firing on the Tri-Bah. What are we going to do?"

"Yen, we need to get out of here. One of those amateurs just might hit us by mistake and those fire lizards are good shots."

Yen got up and dashed to the pilot's chair, working as she sat. Yang turned around, eager to take orders from Victor.

"Send a message home. Tell them, 'They unzipped their pants.'"

"What does that mean?" She asked, more inquisitive than usual.

"Don't worry. Just send it."

"Okay, but you've got to tell us later."

"After sending that, contact the *Gold Rat*. Set up a dedicated channel between us. Configure a display to show her detector data and another one for our own. Then we'll use our combined resources to contact as many of the ships in active combat as possible."

"It's good to hear you working again." She said, flashing him a smile as she manipulated the console.

"Don't confuse panic with a good day's work." He made his way forward and stood next to Yen. She had maneuvered the ship away from the others, but Victor had something more specific in mind.

"Take us into Q-space, somewhere above the planetary plane. We can pop out again, when we want to look around."

"So, we're going to help these people? I think it's a good idea, but it's not like you," said Yen.

"Time for a change." She had no idea how much difference this could make, and Victor wasn't about to explain it now. There was a war to conduct. He rapidly moved back to his cabin and found the red bundle. Throwing back the cloth, he removed the book, held it to his chest and lowered his head. If there was ever a time, he needed wisdom, it was now. The passage that came to mind first had him in doubt.

Thus it is that in war the victorious strategist only seeks battle after the victory has been won

*   *   *

The Group Master paced in a small circle. He couldn't look directly at the envoy for fear of losing control of his anger. "How could you let this happen?"

"I don't care," the Green lizard snarled. "That rodent wouldn't shut up." A medical Tri-Bah finished working on his hand.

"So, you provoked him?"

"They just needed to know their place in the larger scheme of the universe. I explained it to them. They didn't like it. The problem is with them." He touched the binding and moved his claw, checking the mobility.

"You're not in a position to decide that." The Group Master struggled to keep his voice calm. What was wrong with this envoy? Had he no diplomatic training at all? "You should have said nothing. We were talking with them to pacify their anger, not invoke their rage."

"Why are you defending them?" The Green lizard held up his bandaged paw. "I'm the one who's hurt."

"There is no excuse for the human's actions. However, if you tease a serpent, should you complain when it bites you? You got what you deserved." The Group Master turned and walked toward the door.

A slight quiver moved through the ship. The Group Master froze, listening and feeling his ship. He didn't like what he sensed. Even a small vibration in a vessel this size meant something big happened. His aide burst into the room.

"Master, the humans are firing at us."

"High alert." The aide rushed out. The Group Master turned to the envoy. "No chance to avoid fighting them now."

"Will you grant me my earlier request?" The Green lizard asked in a calm voice.

This envoy had arrogance as vast as a bottomless pit. He knew the meaning of this request. As upset as the Group Master was, he now had no reason to refuse it. A ship wide alarm sounded, and another tremor could be felt. Besides, he was late for a battle.

"Yes, you can have the human, I don't want it." the Group Master said, as he left.

CHAPTER 23

"I said, move!" Victor shouted. "You're just a small runabout. You can't stay still and shoot at the Tri-Bah. They're going to . . .," He stopped. Another small white dot had disappeared on the monitor.

"Listen, everyone. A wise general once said, 'he who is skilled in defense hides in the most secret recesses of the earth; he who is skilled in attack flashes forth from the topmost heights of heaven.' In other words, hide until you are going to attack, then surprise them by striking where they don't expect it."

"Ralph Smith here," a voice came from the monitor. "There's no rock to hide behind. We can't keep the pebble fighters away from us long enough to do any attacking. Where do you expect us to go?"

"Q-space. From there, position yourself for an attack. Select a different target every time. Set up your run. Hit them from behind and well within the pebble fighters' perimeter."

"That makes sense. But how the bloody hell are we going to set up a run that close? The ships are moving constantly. We don't know where they'll be by the time we jump back into normal space."

"The *Gold Rat* has been charting the positions of each Tri-Bah ship. Contact them for the locations and they'll help you set up your run."

"Very good. The chaps and I will give it a try. Smith out."

"How about the rest of you?" Victor asked. A dozen other ships were listening to his lecture on tactics. "Can you all do that? Are there any questions?"

"Yeah. Fernando, here. We're a small ship. We have just one tiny energy weapon. I don't think it could frighten a sleeping lizard, let alone do any damage to those big ships. What can we do?"

"I'll bet your ship is very maneuverable because it's small. Am I right?"

"Yes. It's quite nimble."

"Good," Victor said, stroking his beard. "I want you to pop in behind a pebble fighter and target the engines. Get off a few shots and head back to Q-space. They don't consider us a real threat. Otherwise, they'd fly in a protective formation. So, keep them busy and off the other ships' back. And you never know. You may knock out an engine or two."

"We'll try that."

"Good," Victor said.

Over the next few hours Victor watched these few brave humans fighting the best equipped and the best trained fleet in that region of space. He made a note of every ship lost and what they had done.

There were some that didn't do much. He watched a small ship pop into normal space, fire once at the largest Tri-Bah ship, then leave the system. That was all right with Victor. They did what they could. Fear was understandable and normal.

*   *   *

Thomas woke up to a blur of shining gold and deep shadows. Lying in the fetal position, he closed his eyes. At the moment, just breathing felt like a chore.

What had he done?

He realized his arm was wet. He seemed to be laying on some kind of liquid. He feared it was his blood. Any attempt at moving brought a sharp pain to his mid-section. The wound that green bastard had given him throbbed. He needed to get a better look at his side.

Thomas slowly rolled onto his back. Oddly, the floor wasn't flat. Looking down, he saw through his ripped clothing. At least they had the compassion to put a dressing on his wound. The gray bandage clung to his skin and was sealed at all edges.

His head began to clear.

What people had suffered or were in danger because of him? What had he done?

The liquid that soaked his arm turned out to be water running down the side to a drain at the bottom of the floor. Thomas smelled it carefully and risked putting a drop on his tongue. It seemed clean. Cupping his hands as best he could, he scooped up the liquid and took a drink. He also used it liberally on his face and head. The fresh water felt good.

His surroundings came into focus.

Whatever trouble he was in, he could not deny or justify it? He had put himself in danger, but what had he done to the others? What happened to Philip Black and Captain Zavala? Thomas remembered seeing them fall from the blasts of energy weapons. Were they dead? Or could they be in a similar place.

He lay at the bottom of a spherical chamber, less than two meters in diameter. Slowly and painfully, Thomas got to his feet, but could barely stand straight. Not because of the wound, his head was only a few centimeters from the top of the room.

The gold-colored metal had circular indentations, one around a drain at the bottom, another around a hole where the water constantly trickled out. Two more had lights at opposite sides. They glared in the wrong direction, doing little good or shining in his eyes. The same holes for the lights served as portals for the air circulation. And there were other indentations that didn't go anywhere.

How did he get in and how would he get out? Maybe he wouldn't. This could be the last place he would ever know. He pounded on the ceiling with his fists. The confinement closed in.

"Hey! Is anybody out there? Hey. I want to talk to someone. Guard!"

No answer.

He felt shaky in his knees and thought better of standing. The trip down was as painful as the one up. Slowly moving around, he settled into a semi-comfortable position, where his side felt best.

He saw no way in or out. No place to dig, pry or squeeze through. No escape. Thomas was in a cell, wounded and held captive at the mercy of the fire lizards.

*　　*　　*

Victor had finished his lecture on combat techniques to the third group of ignorant, but eager humans.

"Hello, Victor, are you still here?" The picture on the monitor of Ivan's face showed tired eyes.

"Yes. How is it going out there?"

"The *Black Knight* and *Black Watch* have both taken minor damage, but we're good. They've figured out our tactics and are catching on to our rhythm. We need to shake them up or throw them off, anything to change the situation. Have you got any suggestions?"

"You're right, and I have an idea. Let me put something together. I'll get back to you."

Victor had Yang contact some of the smaller ships that had desperately desired to help but were unarmed. He knew it would be risky for them. He also knew that these people had a great deal of determination and courage.

"Listen, everyone," Victor said, with the authority that came natural to him. "As a great general once said, 'hold out baits to entice the enemy.' They don't know you're small and unarmed. You can use that advantage to trick the fire lizards into believing you are a threat. All of you know the term 'riding the inter-phase.'"

"All newbie pilots know about that." A loud voice came through the monitor from the group. "It's one of those things
everyone learns."

"Yes. Manually bringing a ship from Q-space to normal space can be touchy. If the energy vector isn't right, the inter-phase distortion is sustained longer than necessary. You may not pop through at all. It's this distortion that the Tri-Bah are picking up. This is giving them a head start in targeting our ships."

"That doesn't sound good," someone else in the group said.

"No, it's not. What I want you to do is to ride that inter-phase for as long as you can without popping through. This will give those lizards more targets to worry about and take some of the heat off the others."

"That sounds easy enough," another voice said.

"It should be, and the risk will be less than if you were shooting at them. And remember, the longer you can ride that inter-phase the bigger your ship will appear. Ivan, how does that sound to you?"

"That's just what we need. It will throw them off. They won't know what to shoot at. I suggest you start your runs at the rear of their ships. That's where we've been concentrating our effort. Some of us will change our attacks to the side or front."

"And when they get used to that, switch again. Does anybody disagree?" Victor paused for a moment to let them focus on their resolve. There were no answers. "Good. Let's do it."

Chapter 24

"Show me the report from Tactical Analysis," the Group Master said.

The Sub Group Commander told a crew member to have it put on the monitor for the Group Master to study.

"What is your interpretation, Commander?" The Group Master liked to ask his crew questions, because it made them think, not just react. Maybe he would become a teacher after his usefulness as a Group Master to the Tri-Bah Nest had ended.

"It is not what I expected."

"In what way?"

"These Humans are making a good effort. I would even say they show some skill. They have improved as a group since they started. If they were equally matched to us, then we would need more initiative."

"That's a good observation. What of their losses?"

"They were down eight percent, but another group has joined the battle."

"We knew they had more ships." The Group Master thought about both positions. Something caught his eye on the monitor, the fire-to-kill ratio. "Why is our effectiveness so low?" He turned to his subordinate.

"They are small and squirming targets."

"I still expect better from our defensive arms."

"Yes, Group Master. I shall look into it."

"Any word on finding their support ships?"

"Not yet."

"No wonder they are still here. Commander, you must find and remove the support ships from this engagement."

*   *   *

Jolted awake, Thomas, found himself tumbling inside his darkened cell. Water sprayed in and soaked him. What really concerned him was that the water wasn't draining out. It had a strange, but not an unpleasant odor. Perhaps it was soap or a disinfectant, maybe just perfume. As suddenly as it started it stopped. Then the floor shifted, and the liquid ran out.

It was now obvious to Thomas that he had been placed inside a sphere within a sphere. He righted himself. The pain in his side eased off. Grabbing the loose parts of his clothes, he wrung them out as best he could. Again, the room shifted, and the lights came on.

Thomas wondered if this was a Tri-Bah washing machine for their food.

Hot air began to blow in from the two recessed lights. After a few minutes, the room spun once, throwing Thomas off balance. The hot air and tumbling continued until he was almost dry. He smoothed his hair down as best he could without a comb.

The floor shifted once again, and a grate appeared on one side. Light came in and Thomas could see movement. He had an urge to stick his fingers through the small square holes and pull himself closer but thought better of it. If the sphere were to move, he could lose those very same fingers.

"Back away." Came the voice from a translator.

Thomas leaned against the curved wall opposite the opening. The grill fell away. A Tri-Bah warfighter poked his yellow head through the sphere and sat down a bowl in front of Thomas.

"Eat."

"What are you going to do with me?"

The lizard said nothing. He left the sphere, putting the grill back in place.

Thomas smelled the vegetable and protein bits floating in clear broth. The white ones were edible, but the green ones were too sour. He thought the meat tasted like chicken. As if he ever tasted real chicken.

While he ate, he thought about his cell. The indent around the grill was clearly visible. The inner sphere had holes cut in it. As it was spun around, they could be lined up with elements of the outer sphere, lights, water, drain, doors and whatever else the lizards had up their kilts.

The guard opened the grill and reentered the cell. He took the bowl out of Thomas's hand, closed the grill and left without saying a word. Thomas expected the sphere to spin around and cover up the opening. He waited.

After what seemed like a reasonable time, Thomas crawled to the grill and got a better look. He could see the floor below. The sphere seemed to overhang a square pedestal the cell was housed in. Shadows became voices and Thomas returned to the other wall.

The grill reopened and gray spikes poked through.

"Tee, is that you?"

"Hello, Thomas, are you all right?" Red glowing eyes looked him over carefully.

"No. What is going on," Thomas, asked?

"Have they looked at your wound?" The lizard's head barely fit through the opening.

"Yes. They put a dressing on it."

"Good."

"What are you doing on this ship? What are they going to do with me? Can you get me out of here?" Thomas realized that this might be his only chance to be heard by someone in a position to help. He could not understand what influence Tee might have over the Tri-Bah, but he needed to try all his opportunities.

"Have they given you any food or water?" Tees' expression never changed.

"Yes, but what I really want is to get out of here." Thomas had gotten so excited and animated that his side hurt. He moaned and slowly leaned back against the wall.

"Humans are dying," said, Tee.

"What?" Thomas hurt his side again. He wondered if Tee was talking about Zavala and Black.

"They are fighting because of you and the two that died."

"You mean the other humans that are here has attacked the Tri-Bah fleet?"

"Yes, Thomas. I found it disturbing at first. But now I have accepted it as a human reaction. At this point, that puts your species on the border of insane. But I think I understand." There was no way to judge Tees' sincerity.

"I didn't ask them to do that. You can't fault me for their brainless actions. I'm paying for my actions myself."

"Yes, you are, Thomas. Just remember what is written on the temple walls. 'If the vegetation is crushed, tomorrow you will not hear it.'"

"What the hell does that mean," demanded Thomas? "And you think our actions are crazy."

"I didn't say you were insane."

"Look. I need to get out of here." Thomas leaned forward and reached out for one of Tee's horns. He grabbed the front one on the left side. "Can you help me or not?" Thomas was starting to panic.

Tees' red glowing eyes looked up at Thomas' arm. "Do you wish to mate with me?" Came the deep rumbling voice.

"Sorry," Thomas said, quickly letting go of Tee's horns. "I didn't mean to . . ."

"I can't help you, Thomas." Tees' head disappeared out of the hole.

"Wait a minute. What can I do?"

"See you later, alligator." The voice already sounded far away.

The grill was replaced. After a short while, the room moved. The drain reappeared, the water trickled out and the shadowy darkness surrounded him. Thomas was back where he had started. Only his side hurt worse. Thomas pondered what Tee said, 'See you later.' It was the only hope he had left.

CHAPTER 25

Victor was both pleased and disappointed at the humans' hit-and-run assault on the Tri-Bah. The escort ships and amateur warriors were holding their own. The civilians showed a courage and cleverness that he didn't expect but had hoped for.

Unfortunately, they weren't making any difference. Some of the Pebble fighters had been destroyed. A few of the medium sized ships had some damage. But these were insignificant to claim a good showing, let alone triumph. However, winning was not necessary. That was already done and would come later.

They needed to cause bigger damage. He remembered a passage from his beloved book.

That the impact of your army may be like a grindstone dashed against an egg--this is effected by the science of weak points and strong.

A big rock. That's what they needed. Victor knew where to find one. He contacted Captain Patel of the freighter *Wide River.*

"We need your help."

"I don't see how we could help," Patel said.

"You're an ore freighter, correct?"

"Yes. We are hauling twenty-four containers of enriched bauxite. That makes us very sluggish," Patel said. "Also, we have no weapons. We're staying out of the way, just to see how it turns out."

"I sympathize with you. However, you can make a big contribution. It's a matter of using your strength against their weakness."

"I don't see how. Besides that, Representative, traditionally we are pacifists. To be involved with this fighting would be uncomfortable for us. Please don't misunderstand me. We identify with the reasons for your outrage. However, we would have preferred a diplomatic solution."

"I think we all would have chosen that." Victor selected his words carefully. "But we weren't given that opportunity in the beginning when they blew up Bohica. And now thousands are dead."

"I do understand. But killing more will not bring them back."

"I agree. However, the Tri-Bah has been pushing and squeezing us for a long time. They will only stop when they learn we will push back."

*   *   *

Thomas had more time to think than he wanted. The only thoughts that came to mind were regrets. Why did he let his emotions stir him up? He attacked an emissary. Disbelief haunted his guilt. He should have refused to accept this assignment when Director Rodriguez gave it to him. Looking for Bohica sounded so simple. What a mess his stupidity had found. He even doubted his reasons for running for Representative.

As Thomas sat motionless, an overwhelming depression grew heavy on his body. All his fight, sense of justice and resolve melted away. He could not imagine failing worse than this. Holding Charm close wouldn't help this time. He felt like the bottom of a sewer hole.

His prison cell shifted. Knowing what was coming, he didn't care. Tumbling through the wash cycle, Thomas didn't fight it and only moved a little when he dried out. He didn't feel like eating.

The grill fell away and the Green lizard with yellow eyes rose through the hole. A similar bandage to the one Thomas had on his side, wrapped around its left paw covering the snowflake tattoo. Thomas felt cold.

"You humans are such stupid animals," the translator responded to the reptile's hissing.

"Good afternoon to you, too."

"You prove my point. It is the first watch. This is why my race and the Tri-Bah hate your kind so much. You are ignorant, slow and wrong."

"We hate you also." Thomas wasn't in the mood for an argument, but he had nothing left.

"And why is that? The Tri-Bah has made this region of space safe."

"Humans have a fundamental fear of all reptiles. Even so, we try to overcome those feelings by respecting you as a species. We believe that it is the only way we can deal with each other and survive in peace." Thomas truly believed it.

"Don't be naive'. We do not need your respect to survive or flourish." The hisses from the Green lizard sounded angry.

Thomas's curiosity had peaked ever since their meeting in the Bar of Many Welcomes on Fallen. "What does your kind call themselves?"

"You will find out later. We don't want the rest of the humans to know."

"Why not? What have you got to hide?"

"It is none of your concern."

"It became all of our concern when you started killing us. Especially for the ones on Bohica," Thomas found his anger building, but realized its futility.

"You are not dead, yet. You will die, of course, but that will be awhile." The Green lizard leaned against the rim of the opening and glared at Thomas. "Explain to me. Why do all of you carry those primitive weapons?"

"You mean our Kanashimi knifes?"

"Yes."

"We believe that the double edge knife is the icon of man. One edge to create, and the other to destroy. Or you could say, 'a double edge knife cuts both ways.'"

"But why do you carry it."

"It's a complicated story."

"We have time to sort it out," the lizard said, easily. "Please tell me. I want to better understand."

"It's no secret. More than a hundred years ago, we met a species of lizards called the Plume. Have you ever heard of them?"

"No."

"I'm not surprised. They lived further down the spiral arm from here. Everything went well at the start. They seemed friendly enough. Then suddenly they saw one of us. It all turned ugly from there."

"Didn't they see one of you before?"

"Yes. But we have sub-groupings in our species. This particular one is called Asian. There are very slight differences."

"And you still consider them human?"

"Definitely. A long time ago there were some who had problems with other groups. When we met alien species, we realized how comforting it was to have each other. However, for some reason they set off the Plume. They went berserk and killed all of them they could find."

"Why?" The lizard asked.

"We never understood, and they never said. It could have been the facial features or something else. The Plume's just went mad, sought them out, killed them and anyone that got in their way."

"That doesn't make sense."

Thomas couldn't help but smile thinking of Lee-Hope. "Of course, it doesn't make sense. 'Where there is no sense there is no feeling.'"

The lizard studied Thomas for a while with his yellow eyes. "What happened?" He finally asked.

"We analyzed the brutal attacks. They were boarding ships, not destroying them, to get to their victims. Ripping through the passageways and cabins like a demon-ridden storm they searched for their pray. The kill had to be personal. They threw everything they had at us. Attacking every moon, every outpost, every ship, nowhere remained safe. Our people were never a great military power in space. We did what we could. The analysis showed us a need for personally defending ourselves. We rediscovered a long forgotten right given to us by our creator. The right to defend our life."

"So, you used a knife? That seems so archaic."

"Projectile weapons were expensive, dangerous and took training to use. Energy weapons of the time were also costly, unreliable and took even more training to use and maintain. We needed something simple and cheap to mass-produce. So that everyone could be given one quickly. It didn't take long to design an effective blade. It had three parts. Then we stamped out millions of them."

Thomas didn't mind telling the story. There was nothing about it to hide. To him it was long-ago history. In some ways it gave him comfort. The darkest time in human history fit his situation, and perfectly matched his mood.

"There is another aspect in the use of the knife. Our culture has incorporated a discipline into our everyday lives. It is part physical exercise, martial arts and philosophy. It has kept us healthy when we didn't have room to stay fit."

"What does that have to do with the weapon?"

"Moves were incorporated into the routines to train everyone how to use the knife in a defensive and offensive way. Every man, woman and child learned how to use it effectively. We still practice those moves today."

"So, you found a cheap weapon that everyone could be taught to use." The Green lizard tilted his head and studied Thomas. "How did it turn out? Your species is still here."

"The tide changed as we began defending ourselves. But by the time it was over, we had lost two-thirds of humanity. That segment of our people that were targeted went into hiding. They even hid from us, not wanting to hurt any of us because of the Plume."

"That's noble." The expression on the Green lizard hadn't change.

Thomas couldn't tell if the lizard was being sarcastic or sincere. It didn't matter. He would never like the bastard.

"We have no idea where they are or how many are left. We have tried to communicate with them, but they don't want to be found. Humans wear a knife and exercise the moves to remind us of the great sorrow we suffered at the hands of the Plume. In fact, we called the knife 'Kanashimi' which means 'Sorrow'. As for the ones that hid, well, maybe someday we will know where they went. For now, they are only known as The Hidden."

"What happened to the Plume?"

"We believe they're all gone. We killed them all."

The large yellow eyes of the silent beast stared at Thomas. But instead of narrowing the bead, trying to drill a hole through him, the eyes widened as if astonished.

"The rumors about you seem to be true. Humans can lay waste to anything."

Thomas refused to answer.

"I still don't understand. Why did those humans hide after the threat had gone away?"

"I guess they were paranoid," Thomas said, thinking it was a strange question. "Wouldn't you?" Then he realized that the translator on the lizard's belt objected.

"I don't understand what that word means."

"Paranoid?"

Another beep from the translator on the lizards' belt. "Yes."

"It means that *'you are afraid of everything around you.'* Doesn't your race have such a word?"

"No. The closest we have says the opposite."

"You have a word that means *'you are afraid of nothing?'*"

"No. That's not it, either. The word means that *'you make everything around you afraid'*. It's pronounced 'GRRRRR'."

Chapter 26

"Victor," said Yang.

He turned to her.

"There is a lizard trying to contact you," she said.

"Don't tell me the Tri-Bah want to surrender."

"No. It's the spike lizard. Remember, at the meeting."

"The one that Thomas knew personally?" Victor questioned, knowing the answer. His is a rare species. Nobody has ever seen two of them at the same time.

"Yes, that one."

"Let's see what he has to say." Victor waited the short time until the classic red eyes and horns appeared on the terminal. "Good afternoon. Are you the reptile they call Tee?"

"That is my name. Your kind has done well against a superior force. I think some are surprised."

"Thank you for that insight," Victor said. Not wanting to give the true impression, he leaned back and forced himself to relax. "It is very kind of you to offer critiques to our activities here. Do you have any other observations?"

"No. I'm interested in how this situation will play out. But that is not why I contacted you. I don't know if you have the status on Thomas McCormick."

Victor fought the impulse to lean closer to the screen and demand information. "What about Thomas?" he asked calmly.

"I thought you might like to know that he is well." Tees' expression was indeterminate.

Victor sat up in his chair. "Is that so? It looked to me like he was in a dire situation. I don't think any of us could envision him surviving."

"He has. I'm sorry to say that the other two have died, but I talked with Thomas not long ago. He was very animated. He is being held in here." A diagram of a Stone-class Tri-Bah warship filled the screen. Details and information showed the prisoner holding bay and where Thomas was.

"Is this some kind of a trick?"

The image returned to Tee. "This is not deception. My race is neutral in all things. Your dispute with the Tri-Bah and with the events here is completely unimportant to us. We do not get involved."

The screen went blank.

*　　*　　*

Large yellow eyes again studied Thomas as he leaned back in his spherical cell.

"That would make the word 'GRRRRR' the inverse of Paranoia," Thomas said. "That is interesting. Although I can't think how you would use it in a sentence."

"Believe me. There is. It's an old word that came from a more primitive time, but we've found an occasional use for it."

Thomas had been sitting comfortably, resting in the curve of the cell. He thought how surreal the conversation had become. He had not tried to push his luck and ask why Bohica was destroyed and what kind of relationship the Green lizard had with the Tri-Bah. Instead, he and his enemy were discoursing linguistic philosophy in a most civilized fashion.

"I have another subject for you to think about," said the reptile.

"What? Is it your turn to tell me the history of your species?"

"No. Although we will touch on some aspects."

Pain shot through Thomas. He rolled to his left and grabbed his side. Burning agony went from his rib cage to below his left knee. However, it was most intense around his wound. It was like electricity running through his body. As quick as it came, it stopped, except for an ache on the side near his mid-section. Why did it hurt so?

"I'm glad to see that you and your race are suitable." The yellow eyes seemed to laugh.

Thomas straightened himself and looked carefully at his captor. "What are you talking about?"

"Would you like to know how that mystical effect is performed?"

"I'm not sure what you are saying. I don't believe in magic."

The lizard thrust a jade green claw at Thomas and made a fist. "Observe." Then he clenched it tight.

Pain again shot thought Thomas' left side. It quickly subsided. Thomas saw an open claw.

"You do not learn quickly. I will show you again."

The agony returned. "Stop," Thomas said. "I understand."

"You have only begun to understand." The lizard released Thomas from his hurt. "Isn't that a nice touch of mystical justice?"

"You must have put something in the wound to cause that." Thomas wondered what kind of a device was inserted while he was unconscious.

"Yes, but not what you might think. There is a bacterium that lives within the cuticle mites that are common to my race. We are immune, of course. But as with you, many mammals can be harmlessly infected. Each bacterium has a unique connection with the host source. We don't know why or how. It may be related to quantum entanglement. We're not sure. When you distress the mites, it is felt in the infected mammal. Over time, the pain will become more intense and uniform throughout your body. Unfortunately, when I punish you, all of the mammals I've infected are also feeling the pain."

"That's disgusting," Thomas said, not realizing he said it out loud.

"Yes, it is. But we don't mind."

"You did this to me on purpose?"

"Yes. I could just as easily have killed you. I spared you that. The Tri-Bah has given you to me. You will make a nice addition to my household as a slave."

"I would have rather died." Why would the Tri-Bah feel they had the authority to give him to anyone?

"Nonsense. You may be a little slow, but soon you'll carry and fetch like the others. The mystic link, as we call it, allows me to induce pain in my servants to keep them in line. It is quite an evolutionary advantage. We believe that in the primitive past, we would hunt without killing. When it was time to feed, we would render the animal immobile with pain. Then we could eat at our leisure."

Thomas thought how they were like spiders. "Humans don't take well to being slaves. We feel it personally."

"I'm sure you and your kind will adapt and become perfect servants. As soon as this disturbance is taken care of you will be transferred to my ship, and I will return home."

"You mean the fighting that's going on? Is that what you call a disturbance?"

"Yes. Your fellow animals are shooting at the Tri-Bah. They are pitifully outnumbered and lack decent weapons. I don't expect them to last long. They should be rousted soon."

"That's not what I heard. Humans are outnumbered, out gunned and still kicking your butt."

"You don't really believe that do you? When this is over, I can get out of this soggy pit of the universe and get back to the warm walls of home."

"Good riddance to bad rubbish." Agony washed over Thomas. It must have been the wrong thing to say.

"Your training may take longer than I thought. You seem to have a stubborn, if not a slow, mind. We will work on that during the trip home." The lizard released Thomas from the pain.

Thomas couldn't say anything. The ordeal had taken too much out of him. He felt exhausted and wished the Green bastard would leave. Which of the two lizards he talked to were telling the truth? Were the humans fighting well or not?

"I wanted to give you back something to emphasize the point." He placed a small silver ball on the bottom of the cell. "There is your knife. I took it to the Tri-Bah's zero gravity furnace and had it modified. It better suits the situation and has been made harmless. But I still think you should be in 'fear of everything around you.'"

The Green lizard descended out the small hatch of the cell. The door was replaced, and the room spun once. Water trickled out of the wall and ran down to the grate where the shiny ball came to rest. Thomas forced himself to reach over and pick up the sphere of metal.

He felt its weight. Putting it in the water, he washed it clean. Then put it to his mouth and tasted it, stainless steel. The knife had been at his side for most of his life. Now it had gotten him in real trouble. He regretted every hearing the name Bohica.

Thomas had to admit. He was scared. The thought of never seeing Charm again turned his stomach. How could he live without her or even the hope of seeing her? Not that he wanted her here in this situation. That was the one thing that would be worse. He had gotten into public service because he wanted to help protect the people he loved. Now look at the mess it has got him in. Thrown down a dark shaft of hell, to be the devil's servant.

Chapter 27

"Group Master."

"What?" He had watched the metrics of the battle. The on-target solutions were up, but still far below the Subgroup's norm. The tactics of these mammals were good.

"Eight more ships have entered the system," the Subgroup Commander said.

"That shouldn't make a difference."

"These might. They are Surrien combat vessels."

"We don't need any help." A Tri-Bah Subgroup could defeat the humans without assistance. However, help was a gracious gesture.

"They would like to speak with you."

The Group Master made his way to a small terminal. Images of a Surrien ship captain and a priest snapped to life. They were animated.

"Pleasant Time to you," the Group Master said.

"Damn you and your Tri-Bah kind," the priest said. "This unholy action you have taken against Bohica cannot stand without a divine response. We've come to deliver judgment upon you as decreed by the council of the High Chronicle. The desecration of Time will not be tolerated." The priest waved his arms as he talked.

"Stop!" The Group Master shouted. This noise made him angry. "We have no idea what you are talking about. If you are not here to help us subdue hostile elements as defined in our Mutual Protection Contract, then you must leave. This is a Tri-Bah matter and none of your concern." He ended the connection.

"They advance to engage. Their weapons are readied." The subordinate waited for his answer.

The whole situation felt like a broken egg seeping through his paw. There was no way to contain it. "If they fire on us, treat them like the human animals."

*   *   *

Thomas couldn't sleep. His mind was a mess. Thoughts of serving that Green bastard plagued his brain with demeaning images of pain and suffering. He didn't want to go through that. Yes . . . he would survive for as long as he could, but what would that get him? The lizard would find out how easy or difficult it was to control humans. That knowledge would make the next man or woman easier to subdue. He wouldn't survive.

He fiddled with the silver ball that had once protected him. At least that's how most people thought of their knives. The Kanashimi blade had become a comfort in times of danger. The tale of how the knife had saved humans had grown from story to legend, reaching an almost mystical level with humanity. It has become a talisman of security.

Thomas wondered if the belief had gone too far. Could humans protect themselves anymore, from anyone? The times and enemies had changed. Did they need a new weapon to survive? Why were they always barely surviving?

Thomas held up the sphere, resting it between his thumb and two fingers. Had humans become useless to the universe as his knife - round, dull and featureless? He let it drop. Falling from his hand, it rolled around the cell. Splashing through the water, it finally rested on the grate at the bottom, useless as a lump of rock.

"Yes. It is like a rock," he said out loud. Reaching over, he picked up and studied the metal ball with new interest. It wasn't the blade that saved man, but his ingenuity in finding the answer, the solution to his problems. He thought of what it was to be human and free. Armed with new insight, his troubled mind relaxed and he dozed off.

Waking up to the familiar spinning and washing, Thomas couldn't find the metal ball. He felt around blindly and tumbled worse than if he'd stayed still. When the cell finally stopped moving, the sphere was safe in his hand.

The door fell away. Thomas hoped for the Green bastard. His disappointment did not slow his resolve. A bowl, followed by the Tri-Bah guard holding it, emerged into the cell. Thomas felt the stainless-steel rock in his hand. He lifted his arm. Focusing on the three black dots on the bright yellow skull of the lizard, he threw as hard as he could. With the closeness of the target, he had barely let go of the sphere when it hit the mark.

The bowl fell and spilled its content. The guard fell backwards and out through the opening. Thomas didn't hesitate. Fearful that the cell might spin shut at any time, he dove for the door headfirst. His outstretched arms gave way beneath him as he hit the floor and the guard.

Thomas crouched under an overhang of a large box sitting on a pedestal that held his cell. It was only one in a large room contained many rows of these boxes. He got down low and looked around so he could see any feet. It seemed clear.

The guard looked dead. Thomas couldn't tell. Surprisingly, he didn't care. He removed the awkwardly shaped weapon from the still body. Made for the Tri-Bahs' two thumbs and one finger, it felt clumsy in Thomas' hand. He also retrieved the human translator the guard had been using.

Now what was he going to do? There was no way he could escape from the ship, and he couldn't hide forever. Maybe he could do some damage. If they were in a fight with humans, he must try to help. The mere thought of this caused his heart to race even faster.

He quickly moved from one overhang to the next, carefully looking out for other guards. As he neared the end of the row, he heard movement and saw a pair of feet approach. After the guard passed the corner of the overhang, Thomas stepped out from under it and with the awkward Tri-Bah weapon in both hands, he fired. The Tri-Bah guard shook and collapsed onto the floor.

Thomas realized that the weapon was a stunner. It seemed logical that they wouldn't carry anything lethal. After all, what would happen if one of the prisoners got a hold of it? The guard began to move. Thomas shot him a few more times. His hope of running into the engine room and blasting a hole in the inter-phase motivator and blowing up the ship had just turned into a fantasy. It wasn't his day to be a hero.

He limped down to another row, his side hurting. Then made his way to the other side of the large room. Was it his physical activity that irritated his wound, or was it the Green bastard?

An alarm went off. Thomas knew the loud klaxon echoed throughout the ship. Probably someone had escaped. How long could he evade the guards? And if he did, what could he do? He had no real weapons and no skill in sabotage. A long-term escape seemed hopeless.

Thomas heard approaching footsteps. Shooting pain went through his side. He instinctively doubled over and rolled to his side. He knew that Green lizard was doing it to him this time. Darkness encroached on his mind.

CHAPTER 28

Thomas felt himself being dragged. How long had it taken the guards to find him? The pain shooting through his body eased. He forced his eyes open. To his surprise, the two pulling his arms were not Tri-Bah.

"Who are you?" He demanded.

They stopped and knelt next to him. "Can you walk, Mr. McCormick?" The electric voice sounded kind but not familiar.

"I think so." The black and white de-comp armor was the giveaway. How did Yen and Yang get on the ship, and how did they know where to find him? Was this a rescue? Thomas felt pleased, but it didn't make sense. Maybe they thought the others were with him. "Captain Zavala and Philip Black are dead."

"We know," they both said.

"Where did you come from? Is Victor with you?"

"Later. We need to get out of here."

They helped him to his feet. He leaned on one of them to steady himself. Walking was shaky. Every time he stepped on his left foot his side hurt. When they came to a long corridor, Thomas and one rescuer made their way to the right. The other took off running in the opposite direction. What were they doing? Thomas looked back and saw the Igon disruptor removed and ready to fire.

"Wait a minute. You can't shoot that in here," Thomas said to the rescuer, holding him. His panic came through in his voice.

"Keep moving. We must take advantage of the situation and do as much harm as possible."

"But it's an enclosed space."

"It'll do more damage to the ship," the rescuer said.

"And to us as well," Thomas said, but she was not listening. He heard a loud crack. Glancing back, he saw de-comp armor running toward them, silhouetted in orange flames. They weren't going to make it in time.

Pushed up against the wall, Thomas found himself covered by his rescuers. Debris and flames flew by and quickly dissipated. Then they were on the move again.

He could see a curvature of the long passageway. That meant they were close to the outside hull. It explained how the two got in. They could be going back to the airlock they used to enter the ship.

Pain radiated from his wound. Thomas stumbled. If not for the support, he would be on the floor. Was it that Green lizard again?

"I'm not sure how much farther I can go," Thomas panted.

"We're almost there."

As they moved again, weapons' fire echoed up ahead. Thomas expected them to slow down or take a different direction. They moved faster toward the danger. As they got close, Thomas was braced against the wall. The other ran forward to where the shooting came from and joined in.

Were there more than these two? Energy bursts hit around a hatchway on the left, ten meters from where he stood. A burnt, detached airlock hatch lay on the floor. Splatters of molten metal erupted from the wall. He saw return fire from someone at the opening. There were others. The shooter didn't look like Victor. Tri-Bah soldiers must be in the opposite direction.

"Get on the floor," his rescuer said.

Thomas crouched as low as he could.

The action seemed simple. The rescuer quickly walked to her partner. Again, the Igon disruptor smoothly slid into capable hands. She leaned around the corner and pulled the trigger. A small blue line shot out. Thomas heard the crack, then rumbling. The armored rescuer walked back and crouched to cover his body. By this time Thomas felt the heat and saw the glow of orange flames. Then, quiet.

His rescuers helped him to his feet and quickly moved him toward the hatchway. The corridor opened into a large alcove. Dead Tri-Bah soldiers lay everywhere between debris and twisted metal. With no hesitation by his helpers, Thomas found himself guided through the hatchway and into an airlock of a cramped ship. He recognized Kert, Keil and the *Monkey's Fist.*

The throbbing pain in his side increased. Thomas slid to the floor with his back against the bunk bed. Yen and Yang quickly moved to the airlock and closed the inner door. He again heard weapons fire.

"Hang on, we're getting out of here," one of the twins said.

"Wait, they're still out there," Thomas said, pulling himself up. A shooting agony went down his leg and up his back. Again, he wondered if that Green bastard had caused it. The pain eased a little when he bent over. He moved to the airlock and looked out a small window. Yen and Yang were quickly returning fire at a group of Tri-Bah down the passageway.

"Don't worry about them. They can take care of themselves," a twin said.

The floor shifted and Thomas grabbed the door to hang on. The *Monkey's Fist* drifted away from the large Tri-Bah ship. Thomas saw the effect of the air rushing out of the opening. His panic about Yen and Yang and concern for their safety eased. He remembered that the de-comp armor would protect them from the strict vacuum. It was not as good as a full space suit, but they could breathe and be safe.

They both put away their energy weapons and brought out the disruptors. One burst to the corridor wall and the soldiers were engulfed in a brilliant explosion. Thomas couldn't hear it but saw the effects.

When the *Monkey's Fist* had moved a meter and a half away from its dock, a Tri-Bah soldier in de-comp armor came running through the larger ship's airlock and jumped across to Yen and Yang's perch. He hung onto the edge of the opening with one arm and his feet. Grabbing the barrel of the Igon, he struggled to take it from the human. Fortunately, he couldn't reach for his own weapon.

Not wasting time, the other human defender grabbed the trench knife from her side. In one smooth motion, a foot went up the side of the airlock and shoved off toward the intruder. The two humans were synchronized perfectly. The one with the disruptor pulled hard, moving the enemy's arm out of the way and jerking the Tri-Bahs' torso forward. With the blade down and the spikes on the hand guard outward, the knife made contact, driving the spikes into the Tri-Bahs' faceplate. With a quick twist it shattered to pieces. The intruder convulsed and tumbled backwards toward the larger ship.

Yen and Yang recovered quickly. Soon both were shooting thin blue lines of devastation into the enemy ship until orange flames billowed out of its opening and licked at the *Monkey's Fist.*

"Roast them, good," Thomas said out loud.

The space between the two ships grew. The shield of the Tri-Bah warship regained its effectiveness over the open hatchway. A burst from a disruptor spread and dissipated into blue lightning dancing across the massive hull, doing no damage.

The ship continued to fall away from Thomas's view, with the orange flames still erupting from the airlock of the larger vessel.

Surprisingly, Thomas saw a large rectangular shape moving to block his view through his small window. Another one could be seen farther off. Then he saw a third.

As the *Monkey's Fist* moved farther away from the enemy ship, it became clear the objects were large ore canisters. Thomas could see they were on a steady course from top to bottom from his viewpoint. The massive moving boxes descended on the Tri-Bah ship. The targeted ship was trying to move out of the way as fast as it could, but a ship of this size, had the agility of a sack of sand.

Thomas couldn't tell who the winner would be. The first canister easily missed. The second, although close, also failed to hit the mark. Would the Tri-Bah have to deal with the third, despite the fact they were picking up speed? Thomas rutted for the last container.

It all appeared as if in slow motion. Thomas couldn't hear the effect. He imagined metal crushing metal and the shattering of bones as the container full of ore made contact. Slowly the sharp corner ripped into the seemingly thin hull of the monstrous ship.

"Yes." He spoke.

The hide of the beast buckled as the kilotons of brick drove deeper into the curved side. The catastrophic zone grew larger and the deformation of the hull more severe. Thomas couldn't see any slowing in the movement of the container. It looked unstoppable and he was glad.

The Tri-Bah ship continued to pull away. Finally, the two massive bodies separated, but the damage had been done. Debris of metal and flesh poured out of the gaping scar down the side of the enemy ship. The gash went across many decks.

"Good," Thomas said, watching the destructive ballet. Happy with the result, he wondered if he could ever again think of the Tri-Bah as a friend of humanity.

The outer air lock closed, cutting off Thomas's view. He turned from the small window of the inner door and tried to walk toward the stairs of the *Monkey's Fist*. But instead, he doubled over from pain.

CHAPTER 29

The great ship groaned and shuddered as if a predator had sunk its teeth into the hind quarter of the giant beast. The Sub Group Commander shouted orders in rapid fire. He dealt with the evacuation of the affected decks, the mobilization of damage control and maneuvered the ship away from danger.

These animals had no skill, only luck, the Group Master thought. How could they do this? Their good fortune steadily improved. To inflict this kind of damage to a stone class war ship could never come from these rock diggers. What was happening?

The humans called his race cold-blooded. If so, why did his blood boil with anger.

"Commander," the Group Master shouted. "I grow short-witted with these ledge flies. Let's meet with groups one and three. Plot a course for Bah Seven. We'll meet them there."

"Yes, Group Master."

These animals could not stand against the strength of a full group. He must put an end to this.

*   *   *

Thomas slowly opened his eyes. He felt more comfortable. The pain in his side had softened into a mild sensation. He wondered if distance from the Green lizard had diminished the effect. If the Green lizard was right about the bacterial entanglements, it wouldn't make any difference where he was.

Two other people were in the room. Victor talked quietly to another person. Thomas tried to get up from the bed, but only managed a groan, making him the center of attention.

"How's my patient doing?" The stranger studied a small instrument he held.

"I hurt like I fell down a hole." Thomas wasn't kidding.

"Well, you don't look it." The stranger put away the device. "Other than on your side, I find no marks on you. But you're fighting off some strange kind of a bug."

"Yeah, I'll bet those lizards don't clean under their fingernails," said Victor smiling. "This is Doc Hanson, by the way. He came over from the *Danube* to check on you."

"Actually, it was cuticle mites."

"What?"

"Can I sit up?" Thomas shifted his body and moved his legs.

Victor and Hanson helped Thomas to swing around and sit up. His wound continued to hurt when he moved.

"What's this about cuticle mites?" The doctor asked.

Thomas detailed everything he remembered about the conversation with the Green lizard and how a bacterium carried by the mites infected him through the wound. A surprised, disbelieving expression overtook Victor and Hanson when he told them about the pain inflicted through seemingly mystical abilities. Their looks turned to anger, as Thomas explained the lizard's stand on slavery.

"He actually came right out," Victor glared, "and told you that he was taking you back to his home, and train you to be a servant?"

"Yes. He had no hesitation to explain the details to me, or to share the fact that the Tri-Bah had given me to him. Obviously, he thought I would never be speaking to another human."

"What surprises me," Dr. Hanson stated, "is the attitude of those fire-lizards."

"Yes," Victor said. "We have seen a clear shift in their interaction with other species. Not only have they moved aggressively against us, but they have slammed the door on the Surriens. They may be up to something bigger than just Bohica."

"I cleaned your wound as best I could," the doctor said, turning to Thomas. "I also gave you a broad-spectrum anti-infection agent. It should help your body fight whatever they gave you. If it's all right with you, I'd like to take some blood and a skin sample. I know some researchers on Ichorous who would love to find a cure for this."

"Please, take the blood, skin, liver, I don't care. We should be ready for the worst." For the first time since he woke up in the spherical cell, Thomas felt hope. He realized that this was just another challenge to be faced. Humans would not stand by and let other humans fall into slavery.

The doctor took Thomas's blood and packed up his instruments. "I'm sorry we couldn't have met under better circumstances, but I must return to the *Danube*. We're doing our small part as a field hospital."

"Thank you for making a house call. Tell Yang where you need to go, and she'll get you there." Victor shook his hand and Dr. Hanson left.

"I want to also thank you, Victor, for sending your bodyguards to rescue me, even thou it didn't make a lot of sense risking other people's lives."

"Have you heard about not leaving a man behind?"

"Sure, but I thought that was military propaganda to invoke confidence. I never thought it was real. That seems too risky."

"It's for real, Thomas. It's a principle we live by."

"If you say so. I still appreciate it. Now, if possible, I would like to get back to the *Gold Rat* and find out what's going on."

"You can't do that," Victor insisted.

"Why?"

"The *Gold Rat* was hiding in Q-space doing surveillance and helping to guide the attack for the rest of us." Victor sighed heavily. "The Tri-Bah found and destroyed them."

Thomas felt sick. His mind flashed onto the friends he had met and known on the *Gold Rat*. A couple had found good work and a home, in an unfriendly universe. A family building a future in an uncertain time. And he couldn't get his thoughts off a bright young girl who had such grace and charm.

His sadness drew him into anger.

*   *   *

Making his way to the front of his ship, Victor knew that Thomas needed some time to wrap his brain around the destruction of the

Gold Rat. People had an attachment to the ships and crews they spent time with. Thomas would be no different.

Victor sat in the chair and looked at the monitors that had given him a window onto the battle with the Tri-Bah. He reviewed his notes and counted the number of human ships that were destroyed or damaged. Seventeen ships lost and more than twenty severely crippled. There was no way for him to know how many lives were lost. And yet their numbers had grown, and they continued to attack.

Victor could not be more pleased at their courage. When he was very young, he heard a story about two sparrows that attacked a large hawk flying close to their nest. The smaller birds had no chance against the powerful bird of prey. They used their speed and agility to bother the hawk until he flew off. This is what is happening at Bohica.

Now the great Tri-Bah fleet was leaving, and the small human ships continued to buzz around them.

Victor felt a hand on his shoulder. Thomas stood next to him, a far-off look in his eyes.

"Tell me what happened, while I've been out of it."

"Thomas, are you feeling better?"

"Yes, no. I don't care. Please tell me about the fighting. I need to know." Thomas sat in the chair next to Victor and listed intently.

Victor explained the events that had taken place around Bohica after Thomas stabbed the Green lizard. The attacks made on the Tri-Bah ships and as much of the details about the *Gold Rat* as he knew. The strange ore canisters that Thomas saw from the *Monkeys Fist* that plowed into the ship, which imprisoned him, took a little longer.

"What are we doing now?" Thomas asked.

"The Tri-Bah ships are moving back to meet with the rest of their group. That's my guess, probably at Bah Seven. Our faster ships are passing them and hiding in normal space. Then, when the lizards go by, they pop into Q-space and ambush them. They have just enough time to get off a few shots and slip back into normal space. Then they go set up another attack. We'll do that all the way to Bah Seven."

"Why are you doing that? They left Bohica. If you keep pursuing them, you'll have three times the ships to deal with. We should turn around and go back."

Victor could see that Thomas didn't understand. His compassion could be a hindrance. "It's not that easy. The human community is outraged. They have been arriving on the scene from as far away as Ichorous. There is no stopping this."

"We've got to stop the fighting. It's our job and responsibility. These people are not warfighters. Too many have already died."

"I'm very proud of our people," Victor said. "They have fought bravely and with cunning intelligence."

"You make it sound like a good noble thing. Wasn't anything done to stop the violence from getting out of control?" Thomas said with sincerity in his voice.

"I think I understand what you're feeling. You shouldn't concern yourself with the blame for this. It is not your fault. It would have happened regardless. We have been expecting it. I'm surprised it's taken so long."

"I haven't been expecting this. As representatives we needed to do whatever we can to prevent this conflict."

"I think the settlers on Bohica would disagree," Victor said. "We should have protected them and the lives of all humans. You couldn't do that, Thomas. That is why you feel the way you do."

"Oh, and how is that?"

"Guilt, because you think you caused a lot of deaths. Shame, because you didn't accomplish what you set out to do. Sorrow, because friends on the *Gold Rat* died. Anger, because you were put in a cell and treated like an animal. That's too bad. We're in the middle of a war. People die."

Thomas stood up, grabbed Victor and brought him to his feet. Victor saw the anger in his face. Thomas' hands shook.

"You're right. I feel like crap. But you and I are here to see that people don't die. It's our job." Thomas turned white.

Victor saw the glint of cold steel against his friend's neck. His twin bodyguards were quick. One had her Kanashimi knife to his throat and the other stood next to the men with her blade at the ready.

Victor raised his hand. "Please, Thomas, you are not aware of the bigger picture. I think it's time to explain who I am and what is about to happen."

CHAPTER 30

"Sub Group Commander," the Group Master yelled. Around him the noise and activity of the control center continued at the same fevered pitch. "I need you to take us to the staging area. I will be in a conference. Please notify me of changes. It looks like we will be attacked all the way to Bah Seven."

The Group Master turned quickly and left the numbing chaos of war. He needed to calm his anger. Flashing displays and constant chatter hindered his thoughts. The humans were not fighting with traditional maneuvers. They used an illogical approach that would be more harmful to them than to his fleet. Amateurs. They seemed drawn to their own destruction. Let them.

He took the long way around the ship. Stopping at monitors and questioning the warfighters as they performed their duty, he followed the battle. A long corridor turned into an alcove, where he found the green ambassador pacing in front of a large display. The Group Master signaled the two nearby warfighters at this station to move on.

Turning sharply, the ambassador faced the approaching Group Master. "I cannot believe you're running from these cowardly little creatures. Is the great master of the Tri-Bah in charge of an anxious fleet?"

"Of course not," The Group Master felt impressed by the emissary's control. If he had called him a coward, instead of the humans, the green skin would not have survived the conversation. "We are merely changing the dynamics of the engagement to enhance our advantage."

"Spoken like a true politician." The ambassador started to walk away but stopped and looked back. "I'm sorry. The Tri-Bah does not understand the notion of politics, do they?"

"Situations are the way they are. We make determinations based on fact for the greater good, not to make us look better. Individual ambition is unnecessary."

"That has always been an annoying quality about you."

For the Group Master, this was a severely vexing conversation. "It is in our makeup. It allows us to focus on what is important for the Nest."

"And is it important to run away to the safety of your entire fleet?"

Knowing he should walk away; the Group Master took a step forward. "You should discipline your tongues. You could find them tied in a knot." The com device on the Group Master signaled. "Yes, Sub Group Commander."

"We are ready to enter the Bah Seven system. The other two subgroups are deployed as instructed."

"Good." The Group Master was pleased that he didn't have to stay around the emissary. "I want repairs on our hull to start as soon as we are in position," he said, quickly leaving the alcove.

*   *   *

Thomas had a lot to take in. Victor patiently answered all his questions and there were many.

"So, you see, Thomas, it was necessary to hide the truth. We would not be as ready as we are today."

"It doesn't make me feel any better about what happened." Thomas still had a touch of anger brewing in him. "Bohica might have been prevented."

"Yes, you could be right. But you must realize just how paranoid we've been for the last hundred years," Victor said, slowly shaking his head.

"Well, I don't." Thomas straightened in his chair. These new revelations left him surprised, confused and upset. "We have been out there facing all manner of danger, the Uthon disaster, The Sector 22 War and first contact with a dozen unfriendly species."

"I understand, but that's all history. Let the historian's figure that out. Let's move forward. In a short while we'll be at Bah Seven a Tri-Bah prime world. Yang is contacting their leadership to set up a talk.

We hope to have it in an open neutral place. You need to be ready to talk with them again if we set it up."

"What? Why me?" Thomas felt shocked. He couldn't believe what Victor was saying.

"You led the negotiation the last time. All humans know you from that first meeting."

"But I ruined it. I stuck a knife in the other delegate. I'm too emotionally involved and don't qualify. I thought you would do it. You are a representative of such . . . stuff." Thomas really didn't want to return to that situation.

"No, not me. You're what we need, absolutely the right person. Be as angry as you want. We all are. You'll be representing all humanity, all of us," said Victor, patting Thomas on the shoulder.

"I'm not comfortable with this."

"That's all right. Comfort is overrated. Let's get a cup of tea." Victor stood up and moved to another part of the ship.

They had relocated to the small table next to the kitchen. Victor's ship was different, with the shape and size of a private yacht, yet Thomas couldn't quite place it. The inside looked modern and well appointed. But it was sparse, no frills to make it a home. No personal touch or embellishments.

One of Victor's bodyguards approached. "We will arrive in half an hour."

"Are we continuing to press the Subgroup?" Victor asked.

"Very much so. We haven't let up for one moment. They've really surprised me. I expected the fighting to taper off closer to a prime world. However, we continue the attack despite being outgunned. Our ships have been popping out into Q-space and attacking the Subgroup from all directions. Head-on has been the most perilous and from the rear the most beneficial." She looked directly at Thomas. "Their persistence has been commendable. You should be very proud of your people."

"I am," Thomas said.

"I agree, what are the casualties?" Victor asked.

"We've lost twenty-seven small ships and they have lost four. There has also been a lot of moderate damage on both sides. And we have managed to slow the Subgroup down by 20 percent."

"Good," Victor said, smiling. "Do you know how hard it is to slow down a Subgroup?" He asked Thomas.

"No. Not really," Thomas answered, knowing that the question was rhetorical.

"It takes a lot."

"Many people have died to follow us out here." Thomas couldn't help but feel sad.

"And they are very brave to push on," said Victor. He turned his attention to his bodyguard. "Contact all the ships and tell them not to press the fight after the enemy has popped into normal space. We want them to feel relieved, but not comfortable. All the ships are to take up positions around the planet. They are not to engage the Tri-Bah except in self-defense."

"Thomas, you need to get ready. We'll have the *Monkey's Fist* take Yen, Yang and you to the surface."

"I'm still not sure about this," Thomas said, shaking his head.

"Remember, Thomas, you will not be alone. More ships are joining us all the time. We shall also have other surprises in store for them."

The fighting stopped after arrival. It took some persuasion to get the last of the human and Surrien ships to back off. They were reluctant to give the Tri-Bah any kind of a break. Most wanted to carry on the fight despite the odds.

Thomas finely understood that after decades of being corralled and pushed by the Tri-Bah, the collective mind of the humans had snapped, and no amount of destructive force could keep them at bay. But they would stop and talk, for as long as it went well.

Thomas stepped aboard the *Monkey's Fist* followed by the two armored bodyguards. It didn't take long for Kert and Keil to have the ship moving toward the planet.

"Where are we landing?" Thomas asked.

"There is a grassy plain next to a rocky outcropping to the North of their number four city." Keil pointed to a display showing the relative location.

"The rules are simple," Kert said. "Only their delegation and ours set down at the landing site. If anything goes wrong, we're out of there. We'll also broadcast everything that goes on. It will be on a double loop, so everyone sees an unaltered record. So, there is no chance for any deception."

The *Monkey's Fist* buffeted through the atmosphere of Tri-Bahs' seventh prime world. Thomas' fears seemed to rise as the ship lowered to the ground. He realized this could go very wrong. The Tri-Bah could easily wipe them out and continue the fight. Other scenarios flashed through Thomas' head, none of them pleasant. By the time the ship touched the ground, Thomas was as afraid as he had ever been.

He hesitated as they readied to leave the *Monkey's Fist*.

"What's wrong?" asked Kert.

Thomas put his hand to his side. "They destroyed my Kanashimi."

Quickly, four knives were drawn, and their hilts presented to Thomas.

"Thank you," said Thomas unable to hold back a smile. "It's not necessary. We may have to learn to let go and cut away our sorrows. For now, you need them more than I do."

The two bodyguards stepped out first. Kert and Keil would stay in the ship, in case they needed to leave in a hurry. Thomas was amazed at the beauty that met them. The flat plain was covered with a knee-high grass. The stock was a thin pale yellow and topped with a cluster of bright blue buds. The thick, scented breeze kept the grass moving as far as the eye could see. With the light green sky above and the bright blue fields below, Thomas couldn't help but think that this world was somehow turned upside-down.

CHAPTER 31

The Group Master looked over the vast plain stretching before him. Other than the mountains in the far distance, the only landmark was a pointed rock formation jutting skyward. It was known as The Fang. It was as good a place to meet humans as any. He turned to the others.

"Stay at alert, and don't engage your weapons unless fired upon. I want to finish this negotiation and get back on station." The Group Master turned to his officers. "I also want constant communication with the fleet. The humans aren't known as great liars, but they can be tricky."

"How can you give this subspecies any kind of credit? They have no organization or discipline," said the Green lizard.

"That may be, but I have watched and analyzed their fighting. They are brave and savage. We were lucky they are ill-equipped for a challenging battle."

The Green lizard faced the Group Master. "This will not go well for you. Your orders were to put this species in its place."

"I know my orders. I promised you would have access. Remember your place," said the Group Master, turning away from the envoy, gazing at The Fang.

In the cloudless sky overhead one small ship was seen approaching their location. It made a gentle landing. Three humans emerged and walked toward them.

*   *   *

"Namaste, great leaders of the Tri-Bah." Thomas greeted the delegation. He counted eight, four common warfighters, two more that looked like officers, the Group Master and that green devil. The Tri-Bah, he thought, must be tight with that Green lizard's race. Thomas hoped the talk would go well, despite his fear and insecurity.

The Group Master greeted him back. Thomas was glad the translators were working well. He walked through the sea of bright blue buds and approached the delegation. He stopped about fifteen meters from them. His two bodyguards, Yen and Yang were ten meters on either side and behind him. They slowly knelt in the grass with their disrupters at the ready. Thomas felt no safer. In fact, he felt naked to the universe.

"Why are we here?" The Group Master asked. "You wanted to talk, but there is nothing to say."

"Then why did you agree?" Thomas asked.

"Because humans are an annoyance and the sooner, we're rid of you the better this sector will be."

"Is that what happened at Bohica? You got rid of us because we annoyed you? That seems too trivial a reason for this outrage, even from you." Thomas' hot face had nothing to do with the warm breeze.

Taking a half step forward, the Group Master thrust his words at Thomas. "I facilitate instruction from the Nest,"

"Your excuse is that someone told you to do it?" Thomas felt not only his anger but was tapping into some reservoir of long experience with these lizards. "I thought the Group Masters had the power to make policy in their sectors. Make and impose that policy. Or have I overestimated the leash the Nest has on you."

"They also follow orders from their Nest," shouted the Green lizard, butting into the conversation.

The Group Master snapped his head around and yelled at the Green lizard, something the translator disregarded.

"That was good." Thomas smiled to himself. He felt his anger turn offensive. "He speaks and your mouth didn't move. Is he your puppet or are you his?"

"Is this meeting to insult us?" The Group Master asked coldly.

The Green lizard took two steps toward Thomas and clenched his fists, transmitting the symbiotic signal. Pain shot from Thomas' side to his extremities. His knees buckled, and he collapsed on all fours with his head swimming in a sea of bright blue pungent buds and pain.

"Stop that," shouted Thomas' two bodyguards.

The pain lessened and Thomas was able to get up above the blue flowers and face the Tri-Bah delegation. Some of his muscles tingled shaking it off. He could think clearly again.

"Group Master," said Thomas, even more determined, "are you aware of that green one's ability to enslave others by inflicting a wound?"

"Yes. It is an envious talent," said the Group Master. "I'm sure that many more of your species will come to know their talent as you have."

Thomas' blood suddenly ran cold. How could any intelligent species go along with such an insidious practice? Perhaps he had been giving them too much credit. The Tri-Bah may not be as noble as they seem.

"All humans have a special hatred for slavery. We did it to ourselves many years ago. We no longer abide it. In fact, we believe if one man is a slave, we are all slaves. If we are all slaves, we have only one recourse. We will fight until we're all free or dead. We will not tolerate it."

"Big words for a fourth-rate species," said the Green lizard, unable to stay quiet.

"You're right. We can't destroy a planet just like that," said Thomas, snapping his fingers. He wondered if they even understand the gesture. "Only you could be so lizard-quick. But we are also known for destroying planets. It takes a long time for us. We make everything useless. They say our home world is the worst."

"We don't care what you do to yourselves," said the Group Master, now grumpier then angry. "We want you to leave this region and not return. You can't stand against us. Leave while you're free to go."

"Have you checked on the number of ships around this planet?" Asked Thomas. He looked over to Yen on his left. She communicated with Victor.

"Almost two hundred," she said.

Thomas looked back at the Group Master, who was talking with his delegation. He didn't look happy, and Thomas smiled.

"This means nothing," the Group Master said. "You have no chance against us. You have lost here. Leave."

"More of our ships are arriving. I suspect bigger ones are on their way. I'll give you an opportunity to surrender," said Thomas, knowing the Group Master still had the upper hand.

The Green lizard again clenched his fist. Thomas buckled. His knees crushed the blue buds on the ground. He could hear screaming voices. He rolled over onto his side. He could see Yen aiming her disruptor and shouting. The pain finally subsided. It took longer for him to get to his feet this time.

Thomas took two heavy steps toward the Group Master and studied him for a moment. This had to stop. If it happened again, he didn't know if he could continue.

At worst the ship-to-ship fighting would restart. The best thing would be that the talks would stall, and the humans would lose control of the situation. They could lose everything. Too many had died, and many more could die in the future.

"We are not afraid of the few ships you have," said the Green lizard. "I grow weary of this conflict. It is of no consequence."

"You don't have enough ships or firepower to inflict any serious damage to my fleet," continued the Group Master. "Soon my fleet will begin to eliminate all of your ships in this system. They will either leave or be destroyed."

The Group Master lifted his arm and pointed to the Green lizard. "However, if you surrender yourself to the envoy, I will allow your ships to leave. Think about the lives of your species you will save. But do not take long and try my patience. It has grown thin lately."

"Uncle Yoshio," said Yen.

Thomas saw her talking into her com.

As he looked over to her, she gave him a nod and said, "Admiral Kobayashi is here."

Thomas felt relieved.

"Your attempt to negotiate has failed." The Group Master looked smug and defiant. "The only chance to save your kind is to take my offer and surrender."

"I think you misunderstand, and I might have given you the wrong impression," said Thomas, with a big grin on his face. "Because you destroyed a planet, we were mining, and killed thousands of humans, I could see where you might think we should surrender. You might even think that is why I'm here. But you would be wrong. I am not here to negotiate. I am only a humble messenger. The message is that you owe us a planet."

"Is this what you humans call a joke?" barked the Green Lizard.

"Not at all. You took away Bohica. You owe us a planet," said Thomas. He looked around and inhaled a deep breath of the fragrant air. He stretched out his arms and relished the sight of the blue plain and light green sky. "You know what, I really like this one."

"This has gone on long enough. We will not talk again. If your sanity returns, surrender and come with us," said the Group Master. He started to walk back to his shuttle.

"I think we should finish this now," Thomas said. "I can explain it all with one word."

The Group Master stopped and turned around. Thomas knew he had The Group Master by his curiosity and had only to squeeze it a little.

"I learned a new word from that emissary of yours," he continued, his eyes fixed on the Group Master. "But I couldn't figure how to use the word in a sentence. If you can't use a word in a sentence, what good is it? But it came to me that this word stands alone, like 'yes' or 'no.'"

"What is the word," the Group Master asked?

"GRRRRR!" shouted Thomas at the top of his lungs and the sun dimmed in the cloudless green sky.

Chapter 32

"What is that?" Demanded the Group Master, as he looked up at the gray splotch blocking the sun. He turned to the warfighter communicating with his fleet. "Find out what that is."

The Group Master knew the humans were tricky, but this was beyond their capability. Enough talk. He wanted to walk away and leave. They could die for all he cared. However, if this spectacle was a threat to his fleet or to the Tri-Bah of this world he needed to know now.

"Group Master," said an officer stepping to his side. "They are ships. Human ships."

"That can't be."

"But it is, Group Master, more than a thousand war ships. They came into normal space all at once. Taking up position between the sun and our location on the planet has caused this shadow."

Where had these ships been? The Group Master thought back over intelligence reports. There had been no indication that the humans had anywhere near that number of ships. What could he do now? If all the other Tri-Bah fleets were already here, it wouldn't be enough. This would not go well for him. His future and his life were gone. "Check again. I want to know for certain."

"What is going on," demanded the Green lizard?

"Human trickery."

A warfighter ran up to the Group Master and gave him a small claw held display. "Here is an estimate of the quantity and classes of human ships that have arrived. What are we to do, Master?"

The Group Master was stunned. The number and size were beyond comprehension.

"What is it?" asked the Green lizard.

"We're leaving," said the Group Master, quietly turning toward the Tri-Bah shuttle. All was lost.

"I am not leaving here," yelled the Green lizard, "without it." He pointed at Thomas and clenched his fist.

The gray spot in the sky was dissipating as the many human war ships were moving into their assigned positions.

*   *   *

"Thank you, Admiral Kobayashi," said Thomas as he spoke with the commander of the fleet that had arrived. "Your timing was perfect, and the effect was stunning from where we stand." But that was all he could say. Pain flooded his body as he collapsed on the ground, his limbs twitching.

Thomas didn't hear the screaming and shouting at the Tri-Bah by his bodyguards. When Thomas could open his eyes, he was propped up in a sitting position by Yang.

"I need to stand up," said Thomas.

"I think you need to stay down."

"No way, I must do it."

When Thomas got to his feet and could stand on his own, he pointed back at the Green lizard but shouted at the Tri-Bah. "If you are truly a Group Master of this sector, then rid me of this curse."

"Why should I?"

"Count the ships. You're out numbered. More are coming. That should be enough incentive to do anything I ask."

"There are other Tri-Bah fleets in this region who are on their way," said the Group Master.

"You know they are not enough. What happens next is all up to you."

The Group Master turned to his delegation, first to his officers, then to the Green lizard. The translator had been turned off at their end. Thomas understood only the body language and the guttural sounds of their natural speech. The Group Master and the Green lizard were arguing.

Two of the Tri-Bah war fighters grabbed the Green lizard and held him with his arms out. To Thomas' surprise, the Group Master took a weapon from an officer and pointed it at the Green lizard's hands. With a flash and a buzz, the hands fell to the ground. A roar of a wounded animal came from the lizard. The energy weapon must have cauterized the wound. There was no blood. The Group Master changed the settings on the weapon and shot at the ground where the hands had fallen until they turned to flame.

Thomas could feel a tingling throughout his body with an occasional shooting pain. It wasn't long until it settled down. Thomas could not believe what had just happened. As the smell of burning flesh reached Thomas, he realized there was a cure to that green demon's influence. And the Group Master was willing to shoot the hands off a foreign dignitary.

The Group Master gave the weapon back to his officer as the warfighters dragged the Green lizard back to the Tri-Bah shuttle. He turned to Thomas.

"Human, you are free to leave. I suggest we meet at the nearest city." He pointed off in a direction to Thomas' right. "We can resolve this unfortunate incident there," said the Group Master.

The human race won today, and they will win tomorrow. Thomas could only smile.

*　　*　　*

The simple but comfortable chair Major Park had given him helped to relax and recover from the effects of the Green lizard's influence. Thomas' muscles were sore. He felt a chill in the air as he studied the large, jagged rock thrusting its point into the pale green sky. The sun had slipped behind the right side of The Fang. In this landscape, distance was deceiving. Someone had said that it was a half a kilometer high. If that were true, the base would be a quarter of a kilometer wide. That would be a challenging climb.

It had only been a few hours since Major Park had landed with his division of warfighters and the Tri-Bah delegation left. Also, the *Monkey's Fist* had returned to orbit. The large assault shuttles were behind him, along with operations and medical shelters. Two of the medics had looked him over and checked on him periodically.

Thomas watched the activity of the warfighters. The strange looking one-man hover-tanks zipped around in the distance disturbing the sea of blue buds in their wake. They looked so small next to The Fang and seeing them at this distance, they must be fast.

Talks with the Tri-Bah would begin tomorrow at First City. The leader was angry. Thomas couldn't blame him, but he didn't care. Was this the great pivotal moment for the human race? The great Tri-Bah military was forced to back down and surrender. This had never happened in Thomas' memory.

"Mister McCormick."

Thomas turned his head to see Major Park and another warfighter walking toward him.

"This is Lieutenant Vu, she oversees the medical unit and will transport you to the Admirals' flag ship. You will be quartered there until permanent arrangements can be made. Since the Tri-Bah has left, we have been ordered to a different location. I believe you are safe here, so take your time."

"Thank you for being here," Thomas said, and thought about how it will be different tomorrow.

CHAPTER 33

"Namaste," said Thomas to Admiral Yoshio Kobayashi.

"Welcome aboard Mr. McCormick. Are you settling in and are they taking care of you?"

"Your people are doing a fantastic job and quarters are beyond belief. I mean, really. I don't need all that much room."

"Yes, you do. I want you to meet Warrant Officer Moon. He will be your Chef of Staff and direct liaison with me and the fleet."

A uniformed warfighter stepped forward and shook Thomas' hand. "Mr. McCormick, it's an honor to meet you. I took the liberty of putting together a staff support team for you so we can get started right away."

Introductions were made to other uniformed and some non-uniformed individuals who passed Thomas and entered his quarters. When eight or nine had passed, Warrant Officer Moon also entered and began talking with the others.

Thomas turned to the Admiral, "So that's what that big table in there is for?"

"Yes, Mr. McCormick. You're going to need all the help you can get to negotiate a treaty with the Tri-Bah. These are some of our finest people, researchers, lawyers, linguists and strategists. I'm confident that with your help and guidance they can move mountains."

"You're good Admiral. Victor should have warned me about you. I bet you could move some mountains if you put your mind to it," Thomas said, enjoying the moment of a more relaxed situation.

"I move a mountain every day," the Admiral said, putting his hands out, indicating the ship they were on. "This ship is the *Okina Yama*. That translates into *Big Mountain*."

Yes, the Admirals' ship and fleet were huge.

*   *   *

"Namaste," yelled Thomas as he waved to Victor. They had agreed to meet at the Number Four City Transportation Port. Victor was leaving for business on Ichorous and Thomas was hoping he would stay awhile.

The massive structure was typical and very Tri-Bah in its construction. Massive stone pillars holding up a tall flat roof. The open-air Transportation Port was crowded with two distinct groups, lizards that were leaving and humans that were arriving. They were going in all directions.

"Are you sure you can't stay around for a while?" Asked Thomas as he caught up with Victor. "There is so much yet to be done."

"You'll be all right," encouraged Victor, putting down his travel bag. "The Admiral and his people will continue to be invaluable. Besides, I won't be gone that long."

"I still think," Thomas said, "that Rodriguez's hearing will take longer than you think. And I still can't believe that he knew something was going on at Bohica."

"Believe me, Thomas, he knew something. We don't know exactly what, but he's dirty with it somehow. In fact, I've got a suspicion that there is more to it than just him. There may be a lot more people involved. Even if he is innocent, his political standing is gone."

"That is going to take a lot longer to sort out than you think."

"Don't worry about it. I can always come back and visit my friend. In fact, I think I will have to come back, just to unwind from the stress of civilization and people." Victor was grinning.

"Well, with the merging of the Union and the Hidden, the hole political system will have to be overhauled. It will take years to assimilate our two groups back together." Thomas was feeling a little overwhelmed. "I just got elected as a Rep and now I'm out of a job."

"Nonsense don't give me that. Yoshio likes you and he wants you here to help. I doubt there is anyone who will argue with him. You have more to do here then you would ever have to do as a Rep and it's far more important."

"I think you're right about that," said Thomas. "We've got three more transport ships due next week from Tuska. And it's only going to get busier. Already the Admiral has got me working harder than a six-armed jasper."

"And that's why I'm going to recommend that you be appointed governor of this fair rock."

"Don't you dare," Thomas snapped back.

"Oh, yes. I can't think of anyone better suited for the job," said Victor.

"I'm warning you, Victor, don't even joke about that."

Victors' attention suddenly got pulled away at the sound of the loudspeakers. One of the many improvements to the Transportation Port made by the humans.

"That's my ride," Victor picked up his travel bag.

"Hey, why are you not taking your runabout?"

"Didn't I tell you?"

"I guess not," said Thomas, surprised.

"Yen and Yang went off and married Kert and Keil from the *Monkeys Fist*. They're on their honeymoon. The four of them cross married. They took the runabout because it was homier."

"Those poor guys."

"Yea." Victor slowly shook his head.

"At least Keil should be happy. He wanted two wives," said Thomas.

"I've got to go." Victor moved toward the elevator. He stepped in and the elevator moved upwards.

*　　*　　*

Thomas again found himself at the transportation port in the newly named Capital City. It seemed like he went there every day, to see someone off or greet new arrivals or conduct business for humanity. But today was special in his mind, yes, very special. What has seemed like an eternity was about to end. Elizabeth-Charm was arriving at any moment.

The shuttle that Admiral Kobayashi sent to the transport ship settled to the ground. As the people got off the ship Thomas realized that he was excited. When Charm came through the door and stepped onto the ground, he had the urge to run to her, like in the dramas. He thought better of it and decided to walk and meet her halfway. When they met and held each other, he put his face next to her ear and whispered, "I missed you."

"I know," she whispered back.

"I almost forgot," Thomas said, presenting her with a fist full of yellow stocks with bright blue buds at the top.

"They are beautiful and smell great."

"Come, let's meet the rest of the people." They walked back to the small open vehicle where others were waiting.

"This, of course, is Lee-Hope." Thomas couldn't help but notice her saddened face turn bright as she put out her hand to Charm to greet her.

"It is a pleasure to meet you, Mrs. McCormick."

"You are just as Thomas described. I hope we will become good friends."

"I'm sure we will."

Thomas was so glad that Ned had transferred Lee-Hope to another ship that left after the shooting started. When Admiral Kobayashi brought her back, Thomas jumped at the opportunity to look after her. It was a small price to pay back for Ned and Taffa-Lee's help.

"And this is," Thomas introducing the lady sitting next to Lee-Hope, "Marine Corporal Su Nguyen. She has turned out to be a great house manager and nanny."

"I look forward to it," Charm said.

"And this is Warrant Officer Moon."

"Your Chief of Staff," Charm said with a smile. "I understand you have been keeping my husband safe but busy."

"I'm doing my best, Ma'am," he said, "to keep up with him."

"I understand."

"Sir, I do have some news."

"And what is that Officer Moon."

"I wanted to tell you when the whole family was here. We got word from Ichorous. They have accepted the name, Angelica, for this new planet of the Union of Humanity."

As the vehicle erupted with sounds of joy, Thomas couldn't have been more pleased.

EPILOGUE

It was a beautiful night. The stars were stunning in the cloudless sky. The Admiral had several of the Tri-Bah structures converted to homes, offices, and industrial buildings. Thomas and his family were sitting outside of one of the larger homes. He could not believe how nice it was.

They even had something called a fire pit. This was an open fire surrounded by stone that was allowed to just burn. The only purpose was for the beauty of the flames and the warmth.

"You know," Thomas said, turning to Charm, "this fire is going to drive me crazy."

"I know," she smiled back. "I keep thinking about all the oxygen it's using. It's silly, but we're so used to being concerned about those kinds of things."

"It's going to take some time."

"Tell me what is that game with the ball that Su is playing with Lee-Hope?" Thomas thought it was interesting and maybe he could learn how to play it.

"I've seen them play that before, but I don't know what it's called."

One of Admiral Kobayashi's Marines, serving as a house guard came up to them. "Sorry, Sir, but there is someone here to see you."

"At this hour?" Charm objected.

"I'll take care of it," Thomas said. "You watch the fire. Make sure it doesn't go anywhere."

Charm smiled back at him.

Thomas went to the entrance of the house and opened the door.

"Greetings, Thomas."

"Tee, is that you?"

"Yes," Tee said, as he lowered his head to pass through the entry way. "I have brought something of yours."

"What's that?"

Tee opened his two hands holding a silver metal ball and small vile containing a dark substance and offered them to Thomas.

"That's my knife," Thomas said picking up the silver ball. "And that's the sample of Bohica the *Gold Rat* took in Q-space. Thank you, Tee." Thomas was a little stunned. Tee must have gotten them from the Tri-Bah, but why?

"I thought you might want them."

"I do. That's very kind of you. I did not expect to ever get them back. Thank you."

"You are welcome, Thomas."

"Tee, I have a few hundred questions about what happened here and at Bohica. Like why are you here? Who was that green lizard? What are they called? Where do they come from? Are they a threat? Are we going to have more problems with the Tri-Bah? Which one destroyed Bohica? Are they going to do it again? This is intolerable. We don't even know what you call your species."

Tee had his hand opened and Thomas finally stopped talking.

"Thomas, no matter who is talking the translator will always call us 'Spike Lizard'. It will always call you 'Mostly Hairless Mammal with knife'. That is the way it has been designed."

"That's what you call us?"

"Yes, Thomas. As for the other questions, you are not ready for most of them."

"What do you mean," Thomas was getting a little irritated, "we're not ready? What do you know that we don't?"

"Many things, Thomas. I can tell you that we have been around for a long time. Also, your time is coming. Don't be in a hurry. You will be tested in many ways and beyond what you think you can handle. I leave you with advice that your own Melvin Entwhistle has given you. *'You respect the knife that cuts you.'*"

"Thanks Tee, Entwhistle said a lot of things. Now I have another hundred questions to ask. Like, how do you know this?"

"You suggested that I study your literature. So, I did."

"I don't mean about Entwhistle. You said we will be tested and that we can handle it." Thomas's mind was overloading.

"I have seen it before in other species. It is our job to stay ahead of things."

"What things are happening that you have to stay ahead of?"

Tees' red eyes burned into Thomas. "Many things. It will be difficult, but humans are doing well. What has happened at Bohica has set in motion a different line of reality than what was expected. I like it when that happens."

"A different line of reality! What are you talking about?" Thomas was more puzzled than ever.

"I must go, Thomas," Tee said as he turned, went through the doorway and down the path.

"Wait Tee, how can I get a hold of you. I need more answers."

"See you later alligator. Ha, ha, ha."

THE END